The Immortal

Book one of *The Seven Wars*

E. H. Kindred

A Novel Of The Somadàrsath

Copyright © 2012 E. H. Kindred. All rights reserved.

ISBN-13: 978-0615649894 (Sun Hawk Press)
ISBN-10: 0615649890

All characters in this book are fictitious. Any resemblance to actual persons, living or dead, is purely coincidental.

This book is protected under the copyright laws of the United States of America. Any reproduction or unauthorized use of the material and artwork contained herein is prohibited without the express written permission of the author. Please direct inquiries to: E. H. Kindred, P.O. Box 6405, Fredericksburg VA 22403

Published by Sun Hawk Press. All respective logos are © 2012 E. H. Kindred. All rights reserved.

Typeset in: Crimson
Drop Caps in: Preciosa
Display text in: Metamorphous

ACKNOWLEDGMENTS

Many thanks to my family for their continued support of my creative endeavors over the years. My gratitude extends especially to my father, who has been the faithful first reader of every manuscript and revision I have written. Also, I thank the teachers and professors who have read early manuscripts for me over the years, for conversations and encouragement that polished and clarified my thinking on this and many other matters. I wish to thank as well Jackie Reader, who, as her name suggests, has been an invaluable friend to me both as a writer and as a person. Finally, I extend my thanks to my friends, both in person and online around the world, whose continued encouragement and enthusiasm for my work has given me the confidence to share it with the world. I am indebted to you all.

Demon or bird! (said the boy's soul,)
Is it indeed toward your mate you sing? or is it mostly to me?
For I, that was a child, my tongue's use sleeping,
Now I have heard you,
Now in a moment I know what I am for—I awake,
And already a thousand singers—a thousand songs, clearer, louder and more sorrowful than yours,
A thousand warbling echoes have started to life within me,
Never to die.

—Walt Whitman
Excerpted from "Out of the Cradle Endlessly Rocking"

Chapter One

The icy wind howled around the cloaked traveler. The cold was a harrowing, snapping chill that beat against him, blown in swirls by the wind, so that at times it whipped at his back and at others, blew stinging pellets of sleet and snow into his eyes. His horse snorted, puffing out a cloud of steam that was swept away on the wind. Ice clotted in the stallion's mane and clung to the hair around his ankles, making each step through the snow that much harder.

The traveler and his horse were shadows, equally dark, almost lost amid the inky blackness of the night. They passed like specters through the streets of a village. There was no light in the place, not a soul out in the night. Perhaps it was just folded up tight against the storm, or perhaps it had been abandoned for years; it was difficult to tell amid the ravaging blizzard.

The sword on the traveler's back felt heavier than usual. He was aware of its weight pressed against him under the sodden folds his cloak, could feel the strap across his chest shift with each breath, as if it wanted to cinch itself tighter and choke him. He pulled his cloak tighter around him and exchanged his hands on the reins, allowing his right to carry them and freeze for a while, so that his left could thaw against his chest under his cloak.

He did not know if he was close to his destination. He had ridden for two days, sweeping down from the north like the frozen winter that pursued him. The storm had slowed his progress, far more so than the traveler would have liked, to the point of making the land nigh impassable. Had he been an ordinary man, he would have stopped for shelter in an inn long ago, but he was no common man with common purposes and time gave him no sheltering favor.

The traveler did not know this land. Its air was stale and unfamiliar. There were no landmarks to guide his way, and even if there were, the storm would have stolen his view of them. He could only plod onward along the road, hoping, praying that it would not fail him.

Then, out of the darkness, there flickered a light in the distance. As he rode closer, following the road up toward it, the traveler could see the walls by the faint light of lanterns that flickered and sputtered in the merciless wind. Perhaps there would have been a time the sight would bring relief or comfort, but it was not this night. Though he now neared the end of his journey, the traveler had to steel himself, for his arrival here would herald nothing good.

The gates were shut and locked tight against the darkness of the storm. The traveler dismounted and approached, seeing the faint outline of a smaller door set into the left gate. Knowing that his frozen hands would make little sound against it, he unbuckled the sword from over his shoulder and knocked against the wood with its pommel.

There was no sound save the crying of the wind, and so, the traveler knocked again, only to receive the same, howling, nothing. Squaring his shoulders, in no mood for further delays, the traveler drew back his arm and beat at the door until he carved up splinters. At last, the door opened just a crack and a frail beam of light crawled out over the snow.

"Who goes?" asked a voice from within.

"I bear an urgent message for your king," the traveler replied, "Great danger has come to your land."

"You are no ordinary messenger that would have been sent to inform us of anything," the voice replied, "It is the middle of the night, the king is asleep and I doubt he would see you anyway. We do not shelter beggars!"

With that, the door slammed shut and the flickering light disappeared. The traveler stiffened, slinging his sword back over his shoulder, and pulled himself back into the saddle, digging his heels into the stallion's sides. The horse reared up, kicking out with iron hooves to batter at the door before the bar could be dropped back into place. The door surrendered to the stallion with a crack and the traveler urged him on, charging inside, past the short steward who had been knocked into the snow, and into the courtyard. Guards converged on him from all directions, surrounding the traveler in a ring of spear points. The stranger hung his sword from the saddle horn, then dismounted from his horse and held up his hands.

"What business do you have here?" shouted one of the men over the wind.

"Perhaps we might discuss my purpose inside," the traveler replied.

"You are not taking this man into the castle!" the steward protested, having dislodged himself from the snow and scuttled over. "Not after he comes barging in here like this!"

The traveler waited, observing the guards from the depths of his hood, making no further motion.

"Move!" snapped the lieutenant, prodding him in the back with his spear.

The traveler obliged, walking across the courtyard to the keep, the ring of soldiers following him. They passed inside, into the light, shutting the doors behind them. The steward came stomping around to stand in front of the stranger, grousing,

"You can't just—"

The steward recoiled. He found himself looking up into a chalk white face, as pale as the snow that raged outside, with sharp features, which regarded him with annoyance. What held the startled steward transfixed, however, were the eyes that glared down the long pointed nose at him. They were scarlet, a color so fierce that even the rubescent richness of blood could not do justice. There was a deepness to them, as if they had seen far more than any person should, an ancient coldness that made the steward feel as though he stood in the shadow of something great and terrible. The traveler arched a single dark brow and asked,

"*Yes?*"

The low, dangerous edge on his voice bespoke a man not to be trifled with, and one who was already tired of the steward before him.

"Who are you?" demanded the lieutenant.

The traveled pulled back his hood to run a long-fingered hand through dripping black hair before drawing himself up to his full height and turning to regard the soldier.

"Answer swiftly!" the lieutenant ordered.

"I come with a warning to your kingdom," the traveler said. His voice was strong, resonant, though his accent was strange and unfamiliar; flowing and rich, almost melodic in its quality. "There is a danger that has crossed into these lands, one that will wreak its total destruction."

"That something wouldn't happen to be *you* would it?" sneered one of the guards, drawing a jeering chuckle from his fellows.

"On the contrary," the traveler replied, turning his scarlet gaze upon the man, "I am the one who must save you from it."

The soldier quailed under those eyes, not daring to say more.

"Take him to King Tephanis," the lieutenant said.

"You can't be serious!" yelped the steward. "We can't just—"

"Do it," growled the lieutenant.

The steward huffed and looked between the lieutenant and the traveler, who was watching him with impatient eyes.

"This way," the steward grumbled, setting off down the hall.

The traveler bowed his head in thanks to the lieutenant and followed the small man away, the guards walking along with him. The steward was still grumbling under his breath,

"This is absolutely unheard of. There are proper ways to speak to the king. Barging into the castle in the middle of such an ungodly night is in no sense the way to go about it."

They started up a staircase and the traveler glanced up to see several more guards appear at the railing above to meet them. He looked back down to glower at the steward's back, as the man was continuing,

"I don't care who you are or what sort of message you carry, there is nothing so important that can't be—"

The traveler had had enough of this bothersome little man. In one fierce motion, he grabbed the steward by the collar of his coat and hoisted him up to pin him against the wall at eye level.

"Unhand him!" snapped the lieutenant.

The traveler ignored him, snarling instead at the steward,

"I am no messenger, no common knave carrying some diplomatic paper. There are forces at work that your petty mind could never fathom. I will have no more insolence from you. You will take me to your king without another word this *instant*."

The steward gulped, feet dangling above the floor, and his eyes glanced up. It all happened in an instant. The traveler heard the twang of a familiar sound and spun, catching the arrow in a swipe from a single white hand. He snapped the shaft off against the wall and held the point inches from the steward's face, growling,

"Do I make myself clear?"

"Unhand him at once!" snapped the lieutenant, pressing his spear point between the traveler's shoulders.

The stranger obliged, releasing his hold on the steward and letting the man fall back to the floor. With a flick of his pale fingers, the traveler offered the broken shaft of the arrow out to the lieutenant, who snatched it away. Just then, there was a voice from above.

"What is this fracas?"

The guards all snapped to attention as the king appeared at the railing. His eyes fell on the stranger.

"This man demands to speak to you, sire," said the steward.

"Bring him upstairs," King Tephanis commanded and turned from the rail to pass down the corridor toward his study.

The steward straightened his coat and cleared his throat, starting up the stairs once again, leading the traveler behind him. The guards all followed, keeping their spears trained on the stranger, as if expecting him to lunge at any moment. The steward stopped just before the door to the king's study and glanced over his shoulder.

"Sir?" he ventured. "May I ask your— your name?"

The traveler smiled, a look that unnerved the steward even more. The stranger's face was not an unkind one, but a smile seemed hardly fitting to the ancient chill that clung to his presence. The guards and the steward waited in the tenseness, the silence unbroken, until the traveler replied,

"Lask."

Chapter Two

Another broken trap was all he found. For the third day in a row, the young hunter had ventured out into the forest to find his snares robbed of game. At first, he had thought perhaps another animal had found the captured prey before he had, but there had been no tracks, only a few spots of blood. Today, however, there were fresh prints in the new snow.

The young man bent down at the base of the tree to investigate them. They were like nothing he had ever seen. There were two unique types of tracks and he was not sure what to make of them. One was large and wide, cat-like although too big to be a lynx, with points at each toe where long claws had pressed into the snow. The other set had longer toes and a thumb, almost reminiscent of human hand, though much larger and thicker, with the same points from dangerous claws. Whether these prints belonged to the same creature or two different ones, the man did not know, but he was certain that such a creature had never walked these woods before. He glanced up and saw a scratch in the tree, and another, four scratches in parallel lines.

A bead of red dripped into the snow nearby. The hunter looked down at it. Blood. Just then, another drop fell onto his hand. He looked up into the barren branches and caught the shadow of something enormous just before it dropped on him.

The young man's scream was cut off as a large, furry hand clamped over his face, claws digging into his cheek. The other hand pressed into his chest with a weight that made it hard to breathe. He looked up, wide-eyed, not believing what he saw.

It was a monster as from the tales told to children. Tall, sleek, though lined with muscle, it stood over him with a tawny, catlike body, with large paws that planted into the snow on either side of him. A long tail swished back and forth, the air rustling in the feathers that fanned out on the end. Broad wings flared up from its back with pale feathers. Proud hackles puffed out at its chest and continued up its high-held neck to the eagle-like head that looked down at him. Its tall furry ears had flattened back and its dangerous beak pulled back in a smirk while it considered him through sharp, narrowed eyes the color of peridot. A new scar crossed down over the right one.

"Lucky for you, I've just finished my breakfast," it said in a smooth, nasally voice, one that was obviously masculine.

The man's eyes widened even further at the realization that the thing could speak.

"I'm going to let go of you now," he continued, "And you would do well not to scream again, else I will be forced to tear your voice from your throat."

He picked up his hand and the young man lay beneath the monster, panting and terrified. The creature studied him, looking him over.

"You are strong," he noted, "And I have seen you walk this way from the castle. You are a soldier there?"

"Aye," the young hunter breathed, voice unable to go above a frightened murmur.

"Good. That fact will earn you your life this day." The creature released him from under his foot and sat back on his haunches, watching him, as if daring him to run.

The man picked himself up and stood there before him, never taking his gaze from the creature's face, knowing it would be futile to flee.

"What are you?" he asked of it.

"I am a griffin, dear boy." The creature sounded both amused and mildly insulted. "My name is Galator." He paused and narrowed his eyes to ask, "Tell me, young soldier, have you seen a man these past days, a man who is tall and pale as the winter sky with scarlet eyes that burn like fire?"

"Aye," the soldier replied, "His name is Lask."

"Indeed," the griffin murmured. "And do you know the nature of this man? Whence he came and for what purpose?"

"No."

The griffin turned his head, regarding him through a single eye, offering the man a view of the scar that streaked the side of his feathered face.

"How old are you?" the creature asked suddenly.

"Twenty-four," the man replied, wondering why it was relevant.

To his surprise, the griffin laughed, a low chuckle rumbling in his throat and trembling down his sides.

"Why is that funny?" the man demanded.

"Ah," Galator said with a smile, "Because you are but a babe. Tell me, how long do you have before that body begins to wither? How long til that fragile spark of your life goes out?"

"A long while yet, I should hope," the soldier answered. "Fifty years maybe."

"Only fifty?"

The man wasn't sure how to respond.

"What if you could answer instead that you have *centuries* left to live?" the griffin inquired.

"What do you mean?"

"I am in need of a favor, young man," Galator said. "This man who has come to your kingdom means me great harm and so I need someone to watch him. If he leaves, then you must go as well. Follow him, listen to him, learn of his plans. Do this for me and I shall reward you both in gold and in life."

"Life?" the soldier echoed.

"I am kind," the griffin said. "Not only will I let you live this day, but if you help me, I shall see to it that you live for many more."

The soldier eyed the creature, not sure what he meant. Galator's beak twitched back into a slight smile, then asked,

"Have you never pondered the idea of Immortality?"

Chapter Three

Lask had been standing on the battlements since dawn, still and quiet, as if he were a statue adorning the walls. The cold wind tugged at his cloak and hair as he looked out into the clear air of the snow-covered morning, waiting. No one dared to approach him and Lask was aware of the eyes that watched him, the wary, skeptical, frightened looks of the guards and servants that roamed the courtyard. He paid them no mind. At last, a motion in the distance drew his eyes and he caught sight of a green-clad rider emerging from the trees.

Lask descended the stairs, boots crunching in the snow, and approached the gate as the guards there blocked the way of the newcomer saying,

"What business do you have here?"

"He is here to see me," Lask answered them, and the guards parted to allow the rider inside.

The man dismounted. He looked young, with a smooth face and brown hair that was tied back. He clapped a fist over his heart in salute, saying,

"Commander."

"You're late," Lask said. He turned from the gate, motioning for the man to follow him out of earshot of the guards. "I expected you yesterday."

"Sorry, sir, I rode as fast as could, but could not set out until yesterday. The general sends his apologies. The storm slowed our progress considerably."

The soldier reached into his coat and produced a letter, passing it over. Lask opened it, reading,

We are here, perhaps twenty miles north of where you are. Sorry about the delay; that was a hell of a storm and we had no easy time navigating this godforsaken country in all that blizzard. I am here with the sixth Serin, waiting for you. Ecthallia and the second and third Serins are stationed at the Gate, awaiting your orders. Ecthallia has also got half of the seventh Serin out scouring the countryside for any sign of Galator, although progress has not been good, as the snow covered what little tracks there might have been and the scouts are more worried about getting lost in this place than actually keeping track of anything. Capperith stayed behind, as you asked, with the first, fourth and fifth Serins, and as far as I know, they've been rounding up the last of the rebels with little trouble. Assuming that you have had decent dealings with the Letian king, things should be in order. I will remain here until I hear from you.

-Forge

Lask folded the letter with a satisfied nod and said, "Verdin."

"Yes, sir?" said the soldier.

"Return to Forge. Tell him that I will set out northward as soon as I can and meet him there with the small band of mortals the king has assembled for me. I will have further instructions once I arrive."

"Yes, sir."

The soldier saluted once more, then returned to his horse and pulled himself back into the saddle. Lask watched him ride out of the castle, then turned and walked back up to the keep. Once inside, he took the staircase up. He paused at the top, looking at the tapestry that hung on the wall there. He had seen it before, the previous day, but was still intrigued by its presence. It was fine craftsmanship, far surpassing the other weaving-work that hung around the castle. It showed the image of a unicorn, neck arced down as it drank from a crystal clear stream. In the background was a red dragon, resting on a rock amid the patches of sunshine that streamed through the golden leaves. It was a peaceful scene, and one that was familiar in this otherwise foreign place.

Lask did not know how it had come to be in this castle, nor did he have the time to dwell on it. He continued on down the hall and the two guards standing outside the door were all the answer he needed, but still he asked,

"Is the king in?"

"Yes," one of the guards answered. He turned and went inside, then reappeared, saying, "The king will see you."

Lask passed inside, shutting the door behind him. King Tephanis was sitting at his desk and looked up when he entered.

"Good morning," said the king. He motioned at the chair across from the desk, saying, "Have a seat."

Lask obliged, folding his long legs to take a seat in the chair.

"Did your messenger come?" asked the king.

"Yes, sire," Lask replied. "I will be setting out to meet a small contingent of my army as soon as the men you have promised are assembled."

"Good. I have sent for Captain Horace in Gonsing, a most reliable man. Weather permitting, he should arrive tonight and you can set out in the morning. Lieutenant Astikin will be accompanying you also, with eight soldiers to act as your guides and offer information as you need it."

"Thank you, sire."

"Did your messenger bring any news of the creature? Has he been spotted?"

"Not yet, sire. My scouts search for him, but I fear the storm erased what little tracks there might have been, for surely he has been flying to avoid leaving a trail."

"I still don't understand how he could possibly be expected to assemble an army in so short a time."

"Galator is most persuasive," Lask replied. "While it may take time for him to marshal a force large enough to make an attack, I fear each day that passes gives him more time. If he discloses information about our world, offers its secrets, I fear he will have all too easy a time drawing soldiers to his cause."

"And whatever soldiers he marshals here," said the king, "They will be able to kill you in your world?"

"Yes." Lask's expression was dark.

"Then I suppose there is no time to lose."

Chapter Four

Dreselle looked beautiful in the morning sunshine. The cold wind brought a bright blush to her face and Benac had to smile at her as they walked arm in arm through the trees. The pair was strolling the path along the perimeter of Benac's family farm, discussing the plans for their springtime wedding.

"Something small, I should think," said Dreselle, "Neither of us have the means for extravagance."

"We could manage a little bit if you wanted, I'm sure," Benac replied. "After all, we only get married once."

Dreselle smiled at him with an exuberant excitement, saying,

"I think it would be—"

She stopped as a dark shadow passed over them. Benac looked ahead to where a shape shifted in the trees up ahead.

"What is that?" Dreselle whispered.

"Walk back, slowly," hissed Benac, guiding her backward along the path.

Just then, the shape leapt out of the trees, skidding to a halt in front of them, and they could see it for the monster it was.

"What a fine young couple," Galator crooned, "So bursting with life."

Benac pushed Dreselle back behind him, putting himself between his future bride and the creature. Galator let out a low, amused chuckle at the effort.

"I am in need of soldiers," said the griffin, "You, young man, will be a fine addition to my army."

"I'm not a soldier," Benac answered, "I'm not going anywhere with you."

"I think you misunderstand me," Galator hissed.

Flaring his wings, he threw himself forward with a push from his strong back legs, heaving Benac aside and plowing Dreselle down into the snow. She screamed, struggling under the creature's foot, but Galator pressed his weight down upon her, holding her still, as Benac scrambled back to his feet.

"That was not a request," Galator replied, ears flattened back.

"Let her go!" Benac snapped. He had no weapon, but he was prepared to fling himself at the creature anyway.

"Gladly," the griffin answered, "As soon as you agree to leave with me. If you do not..." He tightened his fingers, the tips of his talons digging into Dreselle's shoulders, drawing a whimper out of her.

"Don't hurt her!"

"Then give me your word," said Galator, "I have business in Daeyi and will need all the soldiers I can procure. Fight for me and I will have no need to harm her further."

Benac glanced down to see Dreselle looking up at him from her place in the snow, eyes wet with terrified tears, blood from the nicks in her shoulders staining her dress. Benac glared at the creature, knowing that the griffin could kill him with a swift snap of his beak, and couldn't bring himself to make Dreselle watch him die for her.

"Fine," he snarled, "Let her go."

Galator's face twisted in a satisfied smirk and he picked his paws up, allowing Dreselle to wiggle free. She scrambled upright, saying,

"Benac—"

"Run," he told her.

"But you can't—"

"Run, Dreselle!" he snapped.

She hesitated, then turned and ran, heading back toward the farmhouse, but Benac knew that he and the creature would be gone before she could bring help. He stood, wary, ready to spring if the creature made a move to go after her. Galator did not, instead standing and watching him with satisfied eyes.

"You are wise man," said the griffin, "And such wisdom will earn you a great reward. Now come, we must meet the rest of my men. There is much to do."

Chapter Five

Iask had been given a room in the castle for the night, but he could not sleep. He lay in the darkness for a time, before he got up, too restless to lay still. He paced the chamber, going to the corner to pull on his boots and cloak, leaving the small room to wind his way through the castle corridors, a dark shadow amidst the torchlight.

The guards at the entrance of the keep started in surprise to see him push the door open and head outside at so late an hour. He did not glance at them, sweeping down the steps and across the courtyard, passing out of the castle altogether and into the fields beyond.

The moonlight cast a silvery blue glow on the fields as his boots sank into the snow. He walked out over the frozen ground, coming to stand in the open as a dark silhouette in the moonlight, where he turned his eyes to the heavens.

The stars were bright in the cold, clear air, but they were fewer and less lustrous than he was used to, frozen and unfamiliar. He knew no constellations in them, no point of north or evening star. His eyes wandered among them, seeking a comfort he did not find.

"You made this place," he spoke into the darkness, words fogging on the air, "Yet I cannot feel you here. Do you watch over me, Creator, as you always have? The days of my land have grown dark and we few now find ourselves so far from home. Guard us with your hand, lend us the strength to journey through this strange and dying place. Strengthen my heart for the battle that will surely rage here."

The icy wind tugged at his hair, swirling the edges of his cloak, and the breeze bore no familiar fragrance, only the bitter stale scent of a land forsaken.

Chapter Six

Pulling the dress back up out of the water, Myranda could see that the bloodstain remained on the sleeve. With a frustrated sigh, she shoved it back under, scrubbing at it with a vengeance. She had half a mind to demand a new dress from that horrid Calagan whose blood had ruined the sleeve. If he hadn't been making another bawdy, grabby pass at her, she wouldn't have been forced to break his nose. If only tending his horses did not pay so well, she would not have put up with him at all; although she could not be sure he would keep her around now that she might have permanently disfigured his face, though everyone in the village would agree he deserved it.

A glimmer outside caught her attention from the corner of her eye, and Myranda let the dress sink under the water and straightened to look out the window. It was several hours after sundown, and so the only thing she could see beyond the perimeter of the village was a faint, flickering torchlight. As she watched, another light appeared, and another. Just then, the bell at the edge of the village began tolling out a warning.

Myranda dried her hands, watching as the torches came nearer, not knowing why or who they were. The kingdom was not at war, at least that she knew of, and things had been peaceful between Kwynn and Letiana for years. Gathering her wits, she doused the light she had burning and went back to her bedroom, kneeling down at the edge of the bed. Reaching beneath, her fingers closed around the sturdy oak shaft and she pulled out the spear that was hidden there. It had belonged to her father, from the days when he was captain of the king's guard, and unlike her sister, Myranda had paid attention when he taught her how to use it.

There was shouting and the sound of breaking glass somewhere outside. From the window, she could see the growing orange glow that could only mean fire. A heavy crash sounded from the front where the door was kicked in. Myranda pressed herself back against the wall beside the bedroom door, hearing weighty footsteps and seeing the light of the flickering torch draw nearer.

She did not hesitate. When the man appeared through door, her spear pierced straight into his side. He cried out and collapsed over, and Myranda stood there, stunned, not believing she had taken someone's life. His torch had been dropped and the fires quickly took hold on the blanket that hung over the edge of the bed, breaking her from her horrified stupor. Myranda beat at it, trying to smother it with the other linens, but a familiar voice, shrieking from outside, drew her attention.

Looking out the window Myranda could see that Kirsa, her younger sister, was running from her house, two men hard on her heels. Myranda abandoned the fire, knowing it was useless since the rest of the village was burning as well, and wrenched her spear from the dead man in the floor.

She burst from her house, only to have a pair of rough hands grab her by the shoulders. Myranda spun the spear pole up, cracking the man in the face, and managed to slip free of his grip to go running after her sister. She ran down the street, the muddy ground illuminated by the flames consuming the houses on either side. One was her mother's house, and for a moment Myranda was torn between trying to see if her mother was still inside and continuing after her sister. Kirsa's scream cut through her thoughts and Myranda turned to race after her.

Drawing back her arm, Myranda flung her spear ahead and it found its mark, burying itself into the back of one of the men pursuing her sister. She ran on, jerking it free as she passed, and was drawing it back to throw again when her foot caught on something, tripping her.

Myranda fell over the thing that lay in the road, getting a hand scoured full of gravel and dirt as she tried to catch herself. She scrambled to pick herself up only to realize what she had tripped over.

It was her mother's body. The edges of her dress were blackened from where she had fled her burning house and two black-fletched arrows protruded from her back. Myranda cried out and fumbled, trying to pull her over, but it was clear that her mother was already dead. She let out a horrified cry and could not even fully turn her mother over before a hand knotted in her hair, dragging her up.

Myranda kicked at the man behind her, slamming her heel back on his foot. She punched him in the gut with the butt of her spear and whirled around as his grip let go to stab the point into his chest. Fear was quickly giving way to rage and she planted a foot on the man to heave her spear free of him. Looking around, amid the fires and bodies and struggling forms, she saw her sister just as the man at last caught up with her. He wrestled her to the ground, hands clawing at her dress, tearing it open, fighting back Kirsa's frantic slapping hands.

Myranda took off after her, drawing her spear back to throw, when a wind rushed over her. Something large landed in front of her and she was buffeted back by a strong wing, the force of it throwing her onto her back. Myranda sat up, scrambling back from the monster that stood there before her.

The creature planted a clawed hand over her arm, pinning it down before she could she could raise her spear to stab at him. Myranda lay there beneath him, looking up with amazed and terrified eyes. The griffin fixed her with an emerald-eyed stare that reflected the blazing light of the fires. As he looked at her, Myranda was swept with such a chill, a coldness that paralyzed her, making her feel so small and insignificant. The creature's beak opened, preparing to snap down over her face, when suddenly an arrow struck it in the shoulder.

The griffin let out a grating squawk, head whipping over to find the culprit. He flung himself over at Calagan, who was fumbling for another arrow. Myranda scrambled to her feet and took off running as her employer's scream was cut off by a snapping beak. She ran for her sister, who lay motionless there in the mud.

Myranda flung herself down at her side, drawing up Kirsa's lifeless body with a scream as she saw the fatal red line that spread across her throat. Myranda cradled her half-naked sister against her chest with trembling arms, too late to shelter her, while the screams and the cracking of timbers drowned out the sound of her cries.

Chapter Seven

On the morning of his departure, Lask went out into the courtyard to where a small group of men was assembling. One of the stablehands had tacked his horse, although the stallion seemed to have taken a dislike to the man, prancing and nipping at him.

"He's a spirited one, sir," the stablehand remarked when Lask approached.

"Theramancer just doesn't like unfamiliar hands," Lask replied, accepting the reins. The horse quieted under the pale hand that stroked his neck.

Lask led his horse over to the group of soldiers and a man stepped forward to meet him. He was of average height, with a bit of a belly, and a greying-brown beard and hair.

"Captain Horace, sir," said the man with a nod. "We've been instructed to accompany you by King Tephanis. Your word is our command."

"Thank you, captain," Lask replied. He surveyed the other nine men there, pausing at one to say, "You must be Lieutenant Astikin." He recognized the young man from the night he had entered the Letian castle.

"Yes, sir," the soldier replied.

"Your men know all parts of this kingdom?" Lask asked of the captain.

"Aye, sir."

"And can they keep secrets?" Lask inquired, studying each face there with shrewd eyes.

"Aye, sir, to the grave."

"Good. Then if you are ready, let us set out."

Chapter Eight

Lask rode out in front of the group, flanked on either side by Horace and Astikin, who were the only other two on horseback. The other eight men walked along behind them on foot. After a time, Horace ventured a question.

"The king said that this mission was one of great secrecy and danger. Might we know what it is, sir?"

Lask glanced over at him and saw no point in concealing the matter.

"There is a griffin loose in your kingdom, Horace," he replied. "One which led a rebellion in my land and, having been defeated, fled into yours."

"Why did it come here, sir?"

"To gather an army with which to begin his war anew."

"How is a creature like that going to gather soldiers so quickly?"

Lask glanced at him from the corner of his eye.

"I suppose that would be the secrecy the king mentioned," Horace remarked.

"If the time comes that it needs to be revealed, I will do so," Lask replied. "Until then, I would prefer to keep it if I can."

"Fair enough I suppose," said the captain and he exchanged a furtive glance with Astikin.

"Sir," came a voice from behind them.

Lask looked over his shoulder to see one of the men had spoken.

"I don't mean to interrupt," said the soldier, "But what is that?" He pointed out to the northwest.

Lask looked and squinted against the clear sky, catching sight of a distant red shape against the pale blue. It was a bird, though it flew with labored strokes, as if each beat of its wings was agony. Lask knew it instantly.

He kicked at his horse and Theramancer took off at a gallop, leaving the soldiers standing, confused, behind him. He raced out across the field, just as the bird could fly no more and began to fall from the sky. Lask let go of the reins and planted his feet in the stirrups, standing up and just managing to catch it.

His fingers stained in red the moment he touched it, from the arrow that had pierced through the bird's wing, the blood matting in its feathers. It was a large bird, perhaps the size of a swan, with a golden belly and brilliant red plumage that was tipped in gold. A long, elegant tail draped behind it, though the feathers were crumpled from the fall and being caught. It lay wheezing in his arms, looking up at him through a half-closed gold eyes, which soon shut as it fell unconscious.

"Sir?" came a voice from behind him. Horace had ridden after him. "Sir, what is it?"

"A phoenix," Lask murmured, shifting it in his arms. They were rare creatures, only seven of them in his entire land, and they almost never left their mountain hideaway. He could not imagine what had brought this one so far from home.

"A phoenix?" Horace echoed, as Lask turned his horse to head back to the road. "You mean a firebird like in stories?"

"Much more than just stories," Lask replied. As he returned to the group, he asked, "Does anyone have an extra blanket, spare cloth of some kind?"

One of the soldiers offered him a tattered length of fabric, and Lask took it with a grateful nod, wrapping the bird up in it, both to make the phoenix easier to carry and to protect it from the cold. He held it there in his lap and set off again, quickening the group's pace.

They rode into the afternoon, until they entered a forest and soon caught sight of movement through the trees. Two men on horseback came trotting out to meet them, inspecting the newcomers. Seeing that it was Lask, they each clapped a fist over their heart in salute.

"Commander," said one. "The general has been awaiting you."

"I'm sure," Lask replied. "Show these men to their tents." Turning back to those who accompanied him he said, "I will speak to all of you in an hour."

Lask left the Letian men with his soldiers and rode into the camp. A man with bright red hair, dressed in a rich blue uniform, came stomping over.

"There you are," the general said, taking Theramancer's reins. "I was beginning to wonder." He noticed what Lask carried in his arms. "Holy hell, is that—?"

"A phoenix," Lask replied. He passed the bird down to Forge so he could dismount. "And no, I have no idea what he's doing here or how he got shot."

"I might," the general said. He looked up with a dark expression to Lask, who was slinging the saddlebag over his shoulder. "I've got some awful news, I'm afraid."

"What is it?" Lask asked, taking the phoenix back into his arms and setting off into the camp. Forge walked along with him.

"Last night, Galator was spotted."

"And?" Lask asked, "Where—?"

"We don't know where he went," the general replied as they reached Lask's tent. He followed the commander inside. "But he has marshaled around a hundred soldiers to him already."

"How do you know this?" asked Lask, setting the phoenix down and reaching into his bag that had been brought to fish around for a rag and some medicines.

"Because last night the village of Daeyi burned to the ground."

Lask stopped and looked up, stunned.

"Where were *we?*" he demanded. "Where were our soldiers? Why didn't—?"

"Because we had no idea where he was until it was too late. We had no idea he had already gathered that many. By the time Ecthallia got there, there was nothing left."

"Damn it," Lask growled. He unwrapped the phoenix from the tattered blanket, saying, "Bring me some water. Make sure it's been boiled."

Forge left to do so and Lask started opening a few small pouches of leaves, selecting some to crush between his hands and drop into the bowl. He considered the last bag of them, then opened the saddlebag to reach in for a leather container there. He pulled the lid off of it, revealing a smooth surface of dirt and a thin little seedling that had sprung up there. He had found the seed in the bottom of his saddlebag when he arrived in Letiana and had decided to plant it. Already, the little tree had surfaced and had two tiny leaves on it. Lask decided that the fleeting, mortal nature of Earth must have been speeding up its growing process. He considered it for a moment, then set it aside. While fresh leaves were preferable, he didn't see the point in taking the only two the little sprout had. The dried ones would have to do. He shook them into the bowl. About that time, Forge reappeared, handing him a bowl of water.

"Are the scouts tracking Galator's soldiers?" Lask asked, pouring a bit of the water over the herbs he'd selected to make a paste.

"Of course," Forge replied. "It's too early to have heard back from them though."

Lask nodded, taking up a rag to wet it in the water, and began swabbing clean the phoenix's wing around the arrow.

"At least the mortals didn't skin you alive," Forge remarked, sitting down across from him.

Lask gave a slight laugh.

"Apparently," he said, "King Tephanis's grandfather told him a story that had been told to him by *his* grandfather; a story about a pale man who never aged and couldn't die. Also, apparently this pale man stole a considerable amount of gold from the ancient kings." Lask cast a pointed look up at Forge.

"Malachi, no doubt," Forge said, catching on.

Lask gave a mirthless, affirmative hum. He got a hold on the arrow shaft and snapped it, expecting the phoenix to wake up, but was glad when the bird remained unconscious. He pulled the arrow out and washed the wound, packing the poultice into it before wrapping it tight. As there was still a good amount of the salve left, he scooped it into a small empty jar to save.

"Wonder which one it is," Forge remarked, nodding to the phoenix.

"I don't know. I'll see if I can get him to give me an indication when he wakes."

"So what's the plan then?" asked Forge.

Lask washed his hands in the bowl of water, then sat back, thinking.

"The only way I can imagine Galator has managed to persuade so many to his side already is if he's offered them a chance at Immortality," he said.

"Which is stupid, since he has no way of giving them that."

"The mortals don't know that," Lask replied. "Have Ecthallia and Fildahorr had any trouble at the Gate?"

"No."

"Good. I didn't think Galator would be foolish enough to disclose its location, not when that is his only real bargaining angle with the mortals." He paused, mulling over the situation. "I predict that he will continue to attack mortal villages so long as we hold the Gate so fortified. That's the only way he'd be able to draw our forces away from it.

He knows that we will surely try to defend the mortal kingdoms from his attacks. At least, he will until he has marshaled an army large enough to march on the Gate directly."

"We can't let him get to that point," said the general.

"No, we cannot. That's why it is imperative we track the force he has already, find out where they are meeting, and hope that Galator is there. With any luck, we will find him before he is able to attempt an attack on the Gate and lead the mortals through to Etheria."

Chapter Nine

Lask met with the ten Letian men later that afternoon, taking a seat among them around one of the fires. Forge accompanied him, sitting down beside him to inspect the newcomers. Lask introduced his general and the Letian men in turn, introduced themselves as Horace, Astikin, Viran, Asbern, Sifkin, Fusco, Trasiel, Yothan, Sorek, and Jerryn. Having listed off their names, Horace said,

"If you don't mind my asking, sir, who are these soldiers with you? I have not seen such men in this kingdom before."

"They are soldiers from my land," Lask explained, "Here to help track and slay the griffin. That is where you will help us. We are strangers in this land and will need guides who know the terrain. King Tephanis assembled each of you due to your various knowledge of the land. I am told that you, Viran, have been a scout for several years now and know all sorts of obscure places. Similarly, I hear that Trasiel is an excellent tracker and that Yothan knows the uses of all types of plants. Depending on your skill, I will assign you to various scouting parties to assist in our search or ask you for information as needed. Tomorrow we will make our way northward. Hopefully by then my scouts will have more information."

"How do we know, sir," said Trasiel, "That the griffin is our enemy? I mean no disrespect, but why should we trust *you*?"

"Because my soldiers have not slaughtered and burned any of your people," Lask replied, as if it should be obvious.

"Why can't you fight your war on your own turf?" growled Sorek.

"That would have been my preference," Lask answered, unperturbed, "But the griffin is a coward and is here because he fled."

"From where?" inquired Astikin.

Lask exchanged a glance with Forge.

"We will be keeping that information to ourselves," Lask replied.

After answering (and avoiding) several more questions from them, Lask and Forge took their leave for the evening, leaving the mortals to talk amongst themselves.

"I don't like it," Sorek muttered.

"Something's not right with them," hissed Yothan. "That man is the Devil himself, mark my words."

"Now, now, lads," said Horace, "Lask is right when he says that they have not done us harm. The griffin, on the other hand, has proved himself a murderer. That makes the sides pretty clear for me. Maybe we don't know much about them, but Lask and his men seem like decent enough folk."

"The Devil always seems like a decent fellow," growled Yothan. "That's how he gets your soul."

Chapter Ten

When he parted from the mortals for the night, Lask returned to his tent and heard a low whistle when he entered. He lit a few candles to see the phoenix regarding him with a sharp gold eye and went to kneel beside him. He stroked a hand along his back, saying,

"You're safe for now. Hopefully you will be healed and flying again in a few days."

The phoenix lay his head down, still watching him. Lask shifted over, reaching into his bag to find one of the books he had brought with him. It was small, bound in red leather, with gold letters on the cover that read *The Many Creatures of Our Land*. He flipped past the bookmark in the chapter on griffins, turning back to the heading that read "The Phoenixes." He skimmed over the words there, not reading all of them:

The Immortal

Only seven of them in all the world... act as a communal mind to communicate, only able to speak aloud if all seven are present... Their rare tears can heal the most grievous of wounds and are thought to even be able to resurrect the dead... Their plumes have a number of magical properties... At the end of their life cycle, they will burst into flames and be consumed, only to be reborn out of the ashes... Lask paused, at last finding the information he needed. *Their names, presented in the order of their hierarchy are: Adverett, Terryn, Fressa, Torsenn, Diem, Saryn, and Kymaela.*

Lask glanced up at the phoenix, wondering which of the seven birds lay before him. He decided to read the names aloud, but got no response until he spoke, "Diem," to which he received a short squawk.

"Diem, then?"

A low coo was his answer. Lask set the book aside, tucking it back into his bag, and shifted over to sit nearer to the bird.

"And what are you doing here, Diem?" he inquired. "For I know well that your kind never leave your hideaway in the Arayans except in times of gravest importance."

The phoenix tilted his head, looking up at Lask with a single beady eye.

"As honored as I am to behold you," Lask said, "I cannot help but fear your coming here bodes only ill for me and my task here."

The phoenix's eyes closed and the bird heaved a wheezing sigh. Knowing he would be unable to get any direct information from the bird, Lask poured him a small bowl of water and left him alone.

Chapter Eleven

The next morning, Lask awoke early and looked over to see the phoenix picking at the dressing on his wing. Lask sat up and shifted over beside the bird, saying,

"Here, let me."

Diem settled back and lay still, allowing Lask to take the wing into his pale hands, gently undoing the dressing as he did so. He unwrapped the bandage and rinsed the poultice away.

"It's healed well," he remarked.

Diem watched him through a sharp golden eye. Lask pulled on a clean shirt, telling him,

"I'll go find you something for breakfast. I'm sure you're hungry."

He pulled his boots on and stepped out into cold morning air. Approaching the nearest supply cart, he filled a bowl with some grains and dried fruit to carry back for the phoenix. When he returned to his tent, he reached out to open the door, only to be flown into by a large red shape as soon as he cracked the canvas. The phoenix plowed into him in his fervor to escape, Lask being buffeted by wings and getting a face-full of tail feathers. The grain he had been carrying scattered everywhere. Diem blew past him, wings pumping him into the sky.

"A fine thank you that is!" Lask called after the bird.

The phoenix kept on flapping, never looking back, disappearing into the clouded sky. Lask made an exasperated noise, then went back into his tent to finish dressing with a shake of his head.

He had the camp packed and on the move early, setting out on the road northward while the sun was still low on the eastern horizon. He sent the Letian scout Viran out with the patrol of his own soldiers, along with Asbern, Fusco and Sifkin. The others he kept behind, requesting that they walk with him in the front, so he could ask them all manner of questions about their kingdom. Horace and Astikin were glad to tell him whatever he needed to know, while the other men regarded him with suspicious eyes, not certain they wanted to impart such information to a strange man with a foreign army at his command. Lask could not blame them, but hoped they would prove more forthcoming in the days ahead.

As the sun peaked into noon, a rider appeared in the distance, coming in to meet them. It was the soldier Verdin, who eyed the Letian men as he passed a letter over to Lask. Forge gave him a curious glance and Lask opened the paper to read,

We tracked Galator's men as far as we could, but his force soon split up and retreated in all directions. I can only guess that he wishes to avoid assembling them in one place, so as to remain undetected. I have sent patrols along each of the trails, but I do not want to spread the soldiers too few, in case Galator should choose to ambush them. There were no survivors at Daeyi when we arrived. Perhaps some fled into the surrounding forest or were drafted into Galator's army, for there were a few trails there, but no one alive that we could find. Capperith sent a message through yesterday saying that the last of the rebel force was captured in Etheria and that he and the Serins left under his command can now come to our aid should we need it. Galator has been doing an excellent job of making himself scarce, for as I write this, there has been no other sign of him.

-Ecthallia

Lask passed the letter over for Forge to read and turned back to Verdin who had let his horse fall into step alongside the others, awaiting further instruction.

"Tell Ecthallia to do as she has been," Lask told him. "Keep the patrols fairly large in case they should encounter trouble, but try to keep their passing unseen in the countryside if at all possible. Have Capperith remain where he is for the time being, in case Galator should attempt to return." He looked back to the Letian soldiers and asked, "Which of you knows the landscape of Kwynn well?"

Jerryn raised his hand. Lask looked back to Verdin to say,

"Take them back with you and have Ecthallia send him out to assist her patrols." Lask caught the scouts's gaze and added, "But keep him at a distance."

Verdin nodded, understanding his commander's cryptic instruction. Sorek and Jerryn exchanged glances, but nonetheless Jerryn followed the scout away from the main force, back the way he had come.

Chapter Twelve

The past two days, she had wandered the forest. Myranda passed among the trees, a tattered, forsaken spirit. In the chaos, she had not had time to pull on her shoes and so her feet were bruised and scratched from rocks and brambles, mud-slicked and freezing. Leaves clung to them as she walked, but she had no will to pick them off.

She carried her spear by her side, limp in her hand, the pole dragging in the leaves behind her. She had managed to catch herself a sleeping squirrel the day before, but it had been a small, stringy thing, hardly a meal at all. She was aware of the hunger and the cold, but did not think of them. Myranda had stopped letting herself think about things.

She had wept at first; the hot, frantic tears of a woman left with no one and nothing. As she trudged deeper into the forest, the tears had stopped, giving way to a hollow emptiness, as blank as the fog that curled around the trees.

She had nowhere to go. Myranda found herself totally alone in the wild world. Her father had died long ago and her mother and sister were newly murdered. All of her friends had burned alive or else fallen under the swords of their attackers. Even her horrid employer had been torn to pieces under the fierce claws of the creature. Everything she knew lay behind her in the ashes of Daeyi.

She knelt at a shallow stream, dipping her hand in to take a drink of the icy water. A shadow passed over her and she scrambled back from the water, raising her spear, thinking the creature had been tracking down the last of the survivors. Instead, she saw a bright red bird.

It was large, with long red and gold tail feathers and a crested head. It puffed its chest feathers out, cocking its head at her. Myranda watched it, thinking it looked considerably meatier than the sorry squirrel she had caught the day before. Before she could raise her spear at it, it trilled at her, the long feathers on its head fluffing and bobbing.

It flapped over to another tree, still watching her, and trilled again. Myranda picked herself up, seeing it fly over to another tree, a bit further away, looking back as if expecting her to follow. It squawked at her, almost as if impatient.

Wondering if perhaps the bird was merely a symptom of trauma, hunger and lack of sleep, Myranda decided she had no better option than to follow it as it flew away, leading her off through the forest.

The red bird picked its way from tree to tree, bobbing its head as it jumped and flapped through the branches, glancing down every now and then to make sure she still followed. Myranda trailed after it as the sun peaked into noon and descended on towards evening, wondering why she was bothering. The bird did seem to have a genuine interest in her. There was something intelligent in its eyes that she could not quite make sense of. It was a beautiful creature, the likes of which she had never seen nor heard of, and despite herself, Myranda found herself curious. When it flew off and left her as the sun began to set, she felt a sharp pang of abandonment.

"Hey!" she cried as it took off, flapping straight up into the trees to disappear into the sky.

Myranda looked after it, not even able to tell which way it had gone so to run after it. With a frustrated half-sob, she sank down onto a fallen tree. As her eyes searched the heavens, the tears returned and she wiped them away, angry with herself for believing the bird had been sent to help her.

Just then, there was a sound in the distance and Myranda rose, walking through the trees toward it. The forest thinned out into pasture and she peered around the trees across to a road and the army that walked along it. She stiffened, wondering who they were and if they served the creature that had attacked her. Her eyes fell on the man at their head; a tall, proud man, all in black trimmed with gold, with skin the color of the frost. Myranda watched him, wary, and her heart gave a terrified leap when he looked toward the trees.

Chapter Thirteen

The afternoon progressed without incident and Lask inquired with Horace about a good place to make camp. The captain said there was a fine field perhaps five miles ahead. As the sun began to sink low and they neared the place Horace had spoken of, Lask was looking into the trees off to the side of the road, where a movement caught his eye; a brief glimpse of flapping red wings streaking up out of the forest.

"Go on ahead and set up camp," Lask said to Forge, "I will only be a moment."

"Don't you want to take someone with you?" asked the general. "I don't want to have to be saving you again."

Lask walked his horse over closer to Forge's to say,

"The only thing in this world that can hurt any of us is Galator and something tells me he wouldn't make the mistake of being seen if he were lurking so near our army."

Forge couldn't argue, and so continued on. Lask guided Theramancer off the road toward the trees. The woods were still and silent, no sign of the phoenix that had drawn his attention before. The underbrush was thick in places, so Lask dismounted and let Theramancer wait at the edge of the trees. He walked away into the woods, wary and listening.

Lask scanned the leaves and the last remnants of snow, seeking any kind of disturbance. There was one set of prints, human, that looked recent, so he knelt down to examine them. As soon as he had done so, there was a crack from overhead and he just managed to jump to the side as a spear buried itself into the ground where he had knelt. Before he could even stand or look upward, something dropped out of the tree, tackling him into the leaves.

Lask felt an arm catch around his neck, locking in tight, denying him breath. He threw himself over onto his back, crushing the thing beneath him, and drove his elbow back into its gut. He heard a high-pitched cry next to his ear and kicked at its legs, clawing its arm loose, and slipped away. He scrambled upright, whirling back, drawing his sword to face whatever would come lunging at him. Instead of anything he had expected to see, there was a woman.

"Lady!" Lask exclaimed, startled. He sheathed his sword and knelt down beside her.

She lay on her back in the leaves, fire-hued hair spread out around her head. A tattered dress clung to a shapely, strong form, and her bare feet were smeared with dirt and nicked in places from rocks and thorns. Mud had spattered one side of her fair face and she glared, panting, up at him with forget-me-not blue eyes. She was familiar, like a vision from a long-ago dream, and it made Lask's breath catch in his throat.

"I am terribly sorry, my lady," Lask said, feeling guilty about hurting her, despite being attacked.

"Since when am I *your* lady?" she snarled and made a grab for her spear.

Lask snatched it before she could and tossed it away, pushing her back down with a hand on her shoulder.

"Let go of me!"

She fought herself free of him and got up, Lask rising with her, and she stood there across from him, scrutinizing him with suspicious eyes. Lask waited, hands raised, and allowed her to conduct her study of him. He too, looked at her, expression somehow awed, stunned, as if he could not believe that *she* was at last standing before him.

"What are you looking at?" she demanded.

Lask got a hold of his wits, pushed his surprise down, and said,

"My name is Lask. I am currently leading a small force in pursuit of a creature that has attacked Kwynn. Whatever fiend you believe me to be, I assure you, I am not."

"You're going after it?" she asked, voice quiet.

"Yes."

She sniffed and nodded, then turned, bending down for her spear. Lask stiffened, hand straying back toward his sword, but she did not turn back to him. Instead, she picked up her spear and started off back into the woods.

"Lady," Lask said, stepping after her, "Who are you? Why are you out here alone, unshod, in the cold?"

"What concern of it is yours?" she growled over her shoulder, not turning back to him.

"Because I can help you," Lask replied. "I can—"

"Everything I ever had is *gone!*" the woman snapped, whirling back to face him. "My home, Daeyi, is no more! That *horrid* beast has burned everything I ever loved! How could *you* ever help me? I have no place left in this world. I have wandered these woods like a ghost." She dropped her eyes to the ground, the anger dissipating from her face, leaving such a lost, vulnerable look, Lask went at once and put his hands on her shoulders.

"Come with me," he told her, "And you will wander no more."

She turned her eyes up to him, searching his face, meeting his eyes, wary, frightened, and alone. Lask put an arm around her shoulders, reaching down to coax the spear from her fingers, and started walking, leading her back the way he had come. The woman followed his hand, letting him guide her back to where his horse stood waiting at the edge of the woods. Theramancer snorted at the two of them and Lask laced his fingers to offer her a leg-up into the saddle.

The woman hesitated, looking back into the woods and out across the field, as if looking for a better option. Finding none, she looked back to Lask who waited, patient, for her to make a move. Taking a shaking breath, she stepped forward and let him help her up into the saddle. Lask went to Theramancer's head, taking the reins to lead the horse back toward the road.

"What is your name?" he asked as he walked.

"Myranda," the woman replied. She looked down at the great black horse that carried her, fingers twining in his soft mane. She studied the saddle horn in front of her, the golden hawk's head there, the deep red leather, elegant gold stitching, and looked back up to Lask who walked in front, knowing he could be no poor man. "Why are you helping me?" she asked. "I am just a peasant." She saw his strange eyes glance back at her over his shoulder.

"And what care should I have for what you are?" he asked. "I care not if you are a peasant or a queen. You need help, and I would never think of denying you that."

Myranda considered the back of him; the sure set of his shoulders, the proud way he held his head, and was skeptical that such a man would be helping a peasant so freely. There was something in his eyes when he looked at her, some glimmer of recognition, but he was so foreign to her. She did not know his face or accent and asked,

"Where did you come from?"

"A faraway land," Lask replied, "Much different from here."

"Apparently," Myranda said to herself. She sat in silence for a moment as they traveled through the dusk. Having been in silence for far too long, she had to break it, and so said, "May I ask you a question?"

"Yes."

"Do all the people in your kingdom look like you do?"

Lask glanced over his shoulder at her again, seeing that she looked more curious than frightened, then turned his eyes back out to the road, replying,

"No. Only the men of my family share this coloration."

"Just the men?"

"Family curse."

"*Curse?*" Myranda echoed.

Lask decided to say nothing more, knowing the lack of magic that existed in this world.

"So your family," said Myranda, letting the matter go to break the silence again, "You left them behind?"

"I have no family," Lask replied, "They died long ago."

"Oh. I'm sorry."

"Time has healed the grief I once carried." Lask saw a glimmer further up the road and so said, "Ah. There is my camp."

He led Theramancer up to the perimeter, the guards eyeing Myranda as they passed. Horace approached when he entered, saying,

"Who is that, sir?"

"Her name is Myranda," Lask told him, "She is a survivor from Daeyi."

"Terribly sorry, miss," said the captain with a nod of his head.

Lask led his horse further into the camp and Myranda took in the tall green tents and the soldiers that walked among them. They were clad in green uniforms, a few in rich brown, and she caught sight of one in blue. There was something about them that made her wary, a cold grace, not malevolent, just alien.

Lask stopped and offered a hand to help Myranda slide from Theramancer's back, and he approached a woman dressed in blue nearby, saying,

"Anarra."

"Yes, commander?" said the woman, turning at his voice.

"This is Myranda. She is a survivor from Daeyi. Have a tent pitched for her, see that she is taken a new set of clothes and some water to wash with."

"Of course, sir."

Lask turned to Myranda and told her,

"Once you have settled, come to that fire there." He pointed. "You may share supper with me."

"Thank you," Myranda answered.

Lask smiled, an unexpectedly warm look, and nodded to her, leaving her in Anarra's care for the time being.

Anarra led her to the next row over, calling to one of the soldiers,

"Drake! Pitch another tent while you're at it!"

"Of course, madam."

Anarra entered her tent, motioning Myranda inside. Myranda looked over the things within; the bed roll on the floor, the embroidered blanket that was folded over it, the low wooden table that hosted a few leather-bound books and ledgers, the sheathed sword that rested in the corner.

"Are you a soldier?" Myranda asked of the woman.

"Yes, of course," Anarra answered. She motioned at her blue uniform and the officer's sash across her chest. "And a Serin leader at that." To Myranda's confused expression, she explained, "A division of the army." She opened a bag in the corner, saying, "You look about my size. Try that. It should do until we stop at a town to resupply. We can probably find you something better there." She handed over a simple green dress and some underclothes.

"Thank you," Myranda said, accepting it. She was unaccustomed to such kindness and she studied Anarra with curious eyes. She had never heard of a woman serving in any kind of army and so wondered just what sort of land these people had come from.

Anarra went back outside and went over to one of the carts, Myranda trailing behind her. She watched while Anarra dug through the contents until she produced a pair of boots.

"Afraid these will have to do," the Serin leader said, passing them over. "I can't vouch for the fit, but they'll keep your feet dry and safe from the hard ground."

She then went and filled a basin of water and found a washrag, carrying them with her as she led Myranda back to where one of the soldiers was finishing pitching a tent for her. Anarra placed the water inside and said,

"I'll have someone bring a bedroll and some blankets. If you need anything else, you know where my tent is. I'll be glad to help you."

Chapter Fourteen

Galator had found the caverns by chance and knew at once they would make a fine place to hide his soldiers. Though they were in the cliffs by the sea, they reminded him of the hollow mountain where he had lived for so long in Etheria with the rest of his kind, though Galator would have hardly called it living.

It was in that mountain Galator learned, even as a child, that he was not wanted by his father and would be a burden to his brother. It was in that mountain wounds had festered, and he had later met the man who would become his enemy.

Galator had watched as his father bounded forward, with Ossifer in tow, to greet the young man who had arrived. Galator knew instantly who he must be; the moon-pale hide and scarlet eyes introduced him without needing him to speak his name. It was the one the kingdom had thought dead, the second son of Luke. The griffin's ears perked, listening to his father welcome him into the Griffins' mountain. Galator snorted, knowing his father was making a play for the rising Somadar's favor.

"I am Sabradon, the Rekan of the Griffins," his father was saying, "And this is my son, Ossifer."

Ossifer bowed his black-feathered head.

"It is a pleasure to meet you both," Lask replied.

Galator noticed Lask's eyes shift up, catching sight of him in the shadows and Galator shrank back a bit, not wanting to have been seen.

"That is Galator, my younger son," said Sabradon, a coldness cutting through his sweetened voice. "Pay him no mind. Come, I will have Ossifer show you around."

"I would like that," Lask replied, "Although I wonder if I might have a moment?"

"Of course, sir. The Griffins are honored to have you here; take all the time you like." Sabradon bowed his head, then turned, opening his wings to leap up onto one of the rock ledges. He disappeared into a side cave there, leaving Ossifer with the young Protector.

Galator realized with a certain surprise Lask had turned and was striding toward him. The griffin glanced away, wondering if it was too late to duck back down the corridor. Before he could make an escape, Lask was there in front of him, saying,

"And it is a pleasure to meet you as well, Galator."

"An honor, sir," the griffin replied, bowing his head, ears flattening back with nerves.

"I know well what it is like to be the second son," Lask told him, "The excess heir. And I know too what it is like to have a father and brother who dislike you."

"Dislike is far too tame a term for Ossifer and I, sir," Galator growled. "I am not merely excess, but unwanted altogether, the *accident*. Our mother died giving birth to me, a tragedy my father has never forgiven me for. He did not want me in the first place, and that would have been bad enough for me to endure without the blame of my mother's death upon my shoulders."

"I am sorry."

Galator puffed his feathers out with a certain subdued indignation, tired of only ever receiving sympathy for his situation and never an offer that would help improve it. Almost as if reading his thoughts, Lask said,

"Perhaps you should distance yourself from them. Come down to the south, to the castle. I'm sure I could find you a place there. Perhaps you could act as an ambassador of your race."

"My brother's messenger and mouthpiece?" Galator scoffed. "I think not, sir."

Lask gave a slight smile and Galator was surprised to notice he looked a little disappointed.

"Fair enough, I suppose," said Lask. He nodded, turning to leave, but Galator said,

"Do not lead like my father, young lord. Do not ignore the voices of those beneath you. It will cost you in the end if you do."

Chapter Fifteen

Lask was seated beside the fire, watching Forge stir the contents of the cauldron. He heard the sound of footsteps approaching behind him and looked back to see Myranda.

"Did you get everything you needed?" he asked as she came to sit down nearby.

"Yes, sir," she replied.

Lask gave an amused smile.

"There is no need for you to address me as 'sir'," he told her. "I am neither your lord nor commander."

Forge cast a dubious glance at him. Lask took a moment to observe Myranda. Her face had been washed free of mud and her hair combed out of the tangles and bits of leaf that had snagged in it, leaving it falling in a fiery cascade down her back. Her complexion was clear and smooth, with a faint speckling of freckles across her nose and along her arms. She noticed him watching and asked,

"What?"

"Nothing," Lask said, catching himself and looking away, "You look nice when you're clean."

"Are you saying I was ugly before?" asked Myranda.

Forge snorted and Lask shot a look at him out the corner of his eye.

"Sorry," Myranda muttered.

Lask cleared his throat and motioned at Forge, introducing him,

"Myranda, this is Forge, my best friend and also my general."

"How do you do?" said Forge with a grin. "Soup's almost ready." He paused. "Except I might've burned it a bit." He scraped at the bottom with the ladle, expression guilty. "Sorry about that."

"That's the second time," Lask remarked.

"Capperith usually does this, you know," Forge muttered. "Be happy you're getting cooked for at all in this place."

Myranda glanced at Lask, wondering if he tolerated his officers to make such remarks, but Lask just smiled. He noticed her expression and said, as if guessing her thoughts,

"Forge is like my brother, hence why he can tease me as one."

"It's only fair," said the general with a grin as he ladled the soup into a bowl. He passed it over to Myranda, then dipped another for Lask and one for himself before plopping down across from them.

"Well then," he said to Myranda, "Will we be dropping you off somewhere or will you be sticking around for a bit?"

She hesitated.

"It's a bit early to decide that don't you think?" Lask said with a pointed look at Forge.

"I don't really have anywhere to go," Myranda admitted. "You all are going after the creature?"

"Yes, indeed," replied Forge, "Got a sharp reckoning to deliver on him."

"I'd like to come along then," Myranda said. To the slight skeptical look he gave her, she protested, "I can fight!"

"So you can," Lask muttered.

"Oh, is that where *that* came from then?" asked Forge, motioning to the purple bruise on the side of Lask's neck, just visible above his tall collar.

"Sorry about that," Myranda murmured, shifting as if embarrassed.

Forge snickered.

"You are welcome to accompany us," Lask answered Myranda's initial statement. "But know that we go where there will be much danger."

"I've already been there."

Chapter Sixteen

Lask lay awake that night staring at the darkened canvas above him. His mind was far too restless to allow him to sleep and he had spent what felt like many hours tossing and turning, alternating between pulling the blankets up and throwing them off. Though his chaotic thoughts would not allow him to sleep, he was too tired to sort through any of them.

At length he rose, pulled on a shirt and boots and drew his cloak about his shoulders, getting up to walk out into the cold night air. He paced along the rows of tents, hearing occasional snoring as he passed. The guards on the perimeter nodded to him as he made his way around the camp, seeing that all was well. He paused at the tent that had been pitched for Myranda, and parted the flap just a crack to see if she rested.

"Do you make a habit of looking in on people while they're sleeping?" came a sullen voice from within.

"Ah, but you are not sleeping," Lask replied, embarrassed that she had been awake.

"Yes, and I'm not going to be with a pair of unnerving red eyes watching me."

"Sorry to bother you."

He let the tent flap drop closed again and Myranda sighed in the darkness, knowing she ought to be nicer, but not knowing how to act around him. She lay there, comfortable, but unable to sleep. Whenever she closed her eyes, the flames of that terrible night rekindled in her mind and the screams of the murdered echoed up in her memory. She was exhausted, but feared to sleep, for those horrible thoughts would revisit her dreams whenever her mind lay vulnerable in slumber.

She lay there for a while more, then decided she might as well get up since lying there was so fruitless. If Lask was awake, the least she could do was keep him company after he had seen to it she was so well cared for. Rising, she pulled the dress back on over her slip, but didn't bother with the boots. They were too big for her feet and after the past several days, she had gotten used to walking on the cold ground.

She crossed her arms over her chest as she went out into the night, looking to see if Lask was still lurking around. Not seeing him, she wandered through the rows, but all were quiet and asleep. She approached the large blue tent at the center of the camp that she knew belonged to the commander and drew back the flap to peer inside.

Lask was there within, lying so far on his side he was almost on his stomach. He looked peaceful lying there asleep. The blanket was pulled up to his waist, but she could still see the subtle shape of his hips and long legs beneath. His dark hair was spilled over the pillow and across his shoulders, stark against his paleness. The white skin of his bare back was cast silver in the moonlight that came through the open door and with each deep breath, Myranda could see the coiled muscles just beneath the skin move gently as he slept.

She thought that someone like Lask would have had many scars, but there were almost none. There was only one that she could see, at the top of his left arm, but his back was as smooth and flawless as a child's and looked as if it would be soft to the touch. While she watched him, a wave of unbidden, but sensuous and delightful thoughts came to her— her fingers trailing down the curve of his spine, her palms curling over the planes of strong shoulders, his dark hair falling over her face, smelling of wind and rain, while the sharp point of his nose grazed the line of her neck, the soft insistent whisper of his breath at her ear— thoughts which she savored for a moment, before she caught herself and pushed them away with a mildly disturbed shake of her head.

"And how am I to sleep with an unnerving pair of blue eyes watching me?" came the low, velveteen murmur of his voice.

Myranda bit her lip, embarrassed. Lask pushed himself up and in the wake of her previous thoughts, Myranda caught herself wondering if he were one of those men who slept naked, but a pair of black-clad legs slid out from beneath the blanket. He pulled his boots on and got to his feet, picking up a shirt from nearby. She caught a glimpse of his chest, which looked strong and inviting, before it disappeared under the black fabric. His fingers worked through the strange golden clasps, but he didn't bother with the top ones, so she could still see the lines of his neck and collarbone. He pulled his cloak around his shoulders and swept out to her.

"Sorry," Myranda said, glancing down at the frosted grass.

"It seems we are not so different tonight," Lask answered, "Since neither of us can sleep."

"You seemed to be," she muttered, both embarrassed and irritated from being caught watching him.

Lask could sense her annoyance from the way she glanced up at him, but saw too a fragileness in her expression. He put a hand at her back and led her through the camp, just past the perimeter to a broad oak tree, still in sight, but out of earshot of the guards. He sank down and took a seat beneath it, resting his back against the solid trunk. Myranda hesitated, then took a seat against it beside him.

"Why couldn't you sleep?" she asked.

"Too many things on my mind."

"Me too," she murmured.

They sat there in silence for a moment, looking out at the bright stars that shone on the horizon. A cold breeze rustled in the dead leaves above them and Myranda shuddered and wrapped her arms around herself. Almost without thinking, Lask unpinned his cloak and reached over to wrap it around her shoulders. Myranda looked over at him, as if annoyed, and Lask asked,

"Why do you resent me for trying to help you?"

Her glare faded and she looked down from his gaze.

"I don't," she whispered.

Lask watched her with knowing eyes and said,

"I know what it is like to lose everything that is familiar, to be afraid to get close to anyone else because you fear they too will be torn away from you. I hope you will believe me when I say that things will not be this bad forever."

Myranda looked over at him, unwilling to admit how much the stranger beside her intrigued her. Lask sighed and looked out to the stars for a moment before he closed his eyes and leaned his head back against the tree.

"What are you doing?" asked Myranda.

"Listening," Lask replied. "It is so different here, yet still I take comfort in the wind."

Myranda studied him for a moment, then closed her eyes, mimicking his pose. For a time that neither counted, they sat in silence, hearing only the quiet hushing of the wind in the grass and the gentle trembling of the brittle leaves. At length, Lask opened his eyes to look over and see Myranda as he had been. He smiled to himself as he looked upon her.

The wind blew stands of her hair across her moonlit face in a graceful elegance, trailing across her gently sloping nose that would twitch every now and then from the tickling of one of the strands. His gaze traveled down the soft lines of her neck and throat that was curved in a graceful arc back towards the tree and to the gentle rising and falling of her bosom with each rhythmic breath. He looked down to see her lithe legs with one ankle crossed over the other. Myranda was a strong woman, but her strength did not make her bulky. Indeed, she was a bit skinny and looked like she could use a few hearty meals. He was surprised to see that she hadn't bothered with any shoes, for her feet were still bare, though he couldn't blame her for not wanting to traipse around in bulky soldier's boots. He watched as her toes absently curled over each other as she considered whatever thoughts were running through her mind.

Lask wondered as to the nature of those thoughts. Was she tormented by the memories of the horrible night just days ago, or had she, for this brief moment, been able to escape to a far fairer place? His eyes returned to hers, which were still closed. He wondered if they darkened when she looked on those she loved or if they sparkled when she was happy. He wondered what made her laugh and what kind of life she had lived. Had she been happy? Would she be again?

She must have felt his gaze upon her, for her eyes flicked open.

"What?" she asked, paranoid.

"Nothing," Lask replied, looking back out across the field. "I think I will try once more to sleep. Will you come back yet?"

"I suppose."

He got to his feet and offered a hand to help her up. For a moment she looked at the long pale fingers that invited her and Lask waited for her to make a move. Myranda placed her hand in his and allowed him to pull her up to her feet, pulling her hand away as soon as she was up. She stood there, looking anxious and irritable and Lask couldn't help but think she looked rather comical wearing such a serious expression while his too-large cloak hung off of her and dragged the ground by almost a foot. Lask motioned her on and she trudged off back to the camp, Lask following her with a smile. He walked her back to her tent and she handed his cloak back saying,

"Thank you."

"You are most welcome," he replied, pulling back the tent door for her to enter. "Goodnight, Myranda."

She hesitated for a moment, then replied with a faint smile,

"Goodnight."

Chapter Seventeen

The next morning, Lask received the scouts' report from Forge, all of which proved fruitless. It was as if Galator's small force had disappeared from the Earth. Lask shook his head as he read through the letters, frustrated with the lack of information. He had Forge give the order to break camp, deciding they would continue northward toward the place the griffin was last spotted in hopes of having better information to act on by the time they reached the ruins of Daeyi.

While the soldiers were preparing to leave, Lask tracked down a horse for Myranda and led the mare over to where she was watching two of the soldiers pack her tent, insisting that she didn't need any help with it.

"Did you sleep at all?" Lask inquired when he approached.

"A bit I think," Myranda replied, "Though not much."

"Here," Lask said, handing the reins of the horse to her. "Give your feet a rest."

"Oh, I can walk. I don't need—"

"I insist," Lask replied, with a slight smile that was warm, but final.

"Thank you," said Myranda, reluctantly glad that he had indeed insisted.

Lask left her for a time to tack his own horse, riding up to the head of the column as they set out. Horace and Astikin were there already with Forge.

"What lies ahead?" he asked of them.

"We'll likely reach the town of Masahae this afternoon," said Astikin. "It could be a good place to pick up additional supplies, if needed."

"We shall stop just outside of it then," Lask replied. "I'll send a small party in to buy what is needed. I'd prefer the townspeople not see a whole army if at all possible. No need to arouse undue suspicion, particularly with the attack on Daeyi."

"I thought King Tephanis alerted the Kwynnish king of your presence?" said Horace.

"He did," Lask replied, "But I doubt many of the people outside his castle know of it yet."

Chapter Eighteen

The group parted ways when they entered Masahae, each with their own errands. Lask held back and followed Myranda at a distance, seeing the way she moved through the crowded street. She was likely thinking of her own village, he could tell, as a melancholy shadow descended over her face. She paused to admire a green dress that hung outside of a seamstress's shop, but soon moved on. Lask had seen that she was given a bit of money to get herself a pair of shoes that would fit and a change or two of clothes, but he knew that for a person who had lost everything, it would come as small recompense.

When she disappeared further up the street, Lask approached the shop where she had paused to study the dress there. It was simple, but well made (as far as mortal craftsmanship was concerned anyway) and he thought it would suit Myranda well. He picked it up and entered the shop, going back to where a woman sat at a counter, embroidering the hem of a coat. She glanced up and her eyes widened as she caught sight of him.

"Hello there," Lask said to her, hoping he looked friendly. "How much do you ask for your work?" he inquired, setting the dress up on the table, "And that brown one there." He nodded to another dress that hung off to the side, which he thought would fit Myranda well. Looking back, he realized the woman was watching him as if she expected him to lunge at her. He opened his hand to inspect the coins he had taken from the saddlebag and set few on the counter saying, "While this is not your currency, will three pieces of silver do?"

"Yes, of course," the woman replied, gathering her wits at the sight of the money. "More than do, I'm afraid, as I'm not sure I can supply the difference. Why don't you take a necklace from that table for the lady to make up for it?"

Lask nodded and moved over to inspect the table while the woman folded the two dresses and tied them neatly with a fraying piece of string. Lask inspected the contents of the table, thinking to himself the pieces there were far from Etherian craftsmanship. His eyes found one, a copper star with seven points with a small bead of amber at the center, which he thought would sit nicely around Myranda's neck. He picked it up as the woman came around the counter to hand him the pair of dresses.

"Thank you, sir," she said with a wary nod.

Lask thanked her in return and went back out to the street, tucking the things into the saddlebag before pulling himself back into the saddle and continuing on into the town. He was aware of all the eyes that followed him as he let Theramancer walk along the street, felt their nervous scrutiny on his back. It was not long before he noticed he was being followed by a small handful of people from a distance. Lask couldn't decide why they were following him, but it wasn't long until he realized that a hush had begun to settle over the streets, people stopping to watch him as he passed. Lask had just made the decision to turn back and leave this place to wait for his soldiers outside, when there came, from somewhere out of the crowds to the side, a single tomato.

It struck him in the left side of the face, spraying its juice into his eyes and slinging its soft fruit and seeds across his face, down his neck and over his shoulder. For a moment he could only sit there, stunned, then raised a hand to wipe the splattered entrails of the tomato from his face, shaking the seeds off his fingers with a flick of his hand. He picked the green-leafed top from his shoulder amidst the deathly silence that had fallen and declared,

"Someone in this place has excellent aim. Commendable, truly, but I will be taking my leave. I am going to turn my horse around and be out of this place. I will be no trouble to you."

He pulled on the reins, nudging Theramancer back around the way he had come, only to see his path blocked by five men.

"You're not going anywhere," said one of them. "We've been hearing talk of strange creatures about the kingdom, monsters burning and slaughtering towns."

"Not my work, I assure you," Lask replied.

"He looks like the Devil himself!" shouted someone from the side.

"Burn him!" screamed another.

Lask looked toward the source, surprised and insulted.

"I promise you, I mean you no harm," he said to the men in his path, "And if you will let me, I will leave your town this instant and trouble you no more."

"We can't allow that," said one of the men, "Not when you might move on to another."

They stepped forward and Theramancer snorted, sidestepping away from them, only to find that the crowd had edged closer blocking the way. They grabbed at the horse's reins and the stallion reared up with a shrill scream, kicking out at them with ironclad hooves. When he came crashing back down to all fours, Lask drew his sword from over his shoulder, holding its dangerous blade out at the men before him.

"HEY!" came a shout from over the noise.

Forge shoved his way through the crowd, a group of Etherian soldiers in his wake, and they surrounded their commander, daring another villager to touch him.

"Now if you're finished," Forge snapped at the men in front of them, "We're going to be on our way. If you think of taking a notion to stop us, you're going to have a big problem on your hands."

The man in front regarded him with disdainful eyes, but after a moment stepped out of the way, growling,

"Be gone with you and don't ever set foot here again."

Forge barged past him and Lask followed, his soldiers walking along on either side, just to ensure the townsfolk kept their distance. They passed out of the gate and out onto the road once more.

"People," muttered Forge as they walked, "Honestly." He glanced back to see Lask wiping the rest of the tomato off his face.

"I have never been so insulted in my life," Lask snarled. Indeed, no one in Etheria would have dared to do such a thing to him and certainly not in public. He glanced skyward. "There are still several hours of good daylight left. We will be well clear of this place by nightfall."

"I thought—"

"We're moving on," Lask said. "I don't want a bunch of peasants with pitchforks trying their hand with us tonight."

Forge conceded, knowing better than to argue when his friend's dignity had been compromised.

"Were you able to get anything?" Lask asked after a moment.

"Yes. I had just sent a full wagon back when I heard the commotion."

"Did Myranda—?"

"She went back with the wagon."

"Good."

They returned to the place where the army waited. Not much of the camp had been set up yet, and as soon as they returned, Forge started calling to prepare to move out. While he did so, Lask dismounted and found a bit of water to wash the sticky tomato residue off his face, still picking seeds out of his hair and from the folds of his cloak. He glanced up to see Myranda approaching, glad that he had gotten his face clean before she could see him.

"What happened?" she asked.

"Tomato," Lask growled.

Myranda looked confused for a moment, then caught sight of a few pieces of fruit still clinging to him

"Those rotten bastards," she exclaimed, reaching to pick the pieces out of his hair.

Lask looked at her, surprised, and Myranda withdrew her hand saying,

"Sorry."

"No, I was more startled to hear such a lovely lady swear so vehemently," he remarked.

Myranda looked guilty for a moment, but then said,

"Well, in that case..." She reached up to pluck a few more seeds out of his dark hair.

Chapter Nineteen

Lask had his soldiers travel on until sunset, putting a decent distance between them and Masahae. Once he had put his things in his tent, Lask took up the clothes he gotten for Myranda earlier in the day and carried them over to her tent, approaching as she was coming out. She smiled at him, and Lask had to admit that he was glad she seemed happy to see him. He offered her the small bundle.

"I took the liberty of picking up a few things for you before I was run out of Masahae," he said. "I thought you might like a few more things than what you were able to get with whatever Forge gave you to spend." He gave a crooked smile. "I know he can be a bit thrifty."

"Oh!" Myranda exclaimed, seeing just what was folded there for her. "Oh, you didn't have to. I did alright with what I had."

"But I wanted to," Lask replied, and indeed there was a

warm feeling in his chest at the thought of taking care of her. "I thought they would look nice on you."

He was a bit surprised to see Myranda blush.

"Thank you," she said, looking uncharacteristically shy.

"Of course." He put a hand on her shoulder. "We'll be having dinner soon. I hope you'll join us."

Myranda nodded and he left her alone for a while. She reappeared later in the evening and accepted the stew Forge offered her. After they had eaten, the general left them alone. Myranda lingered by the fire next to Lask and was more talkative than she had been the previous night. Lask sat and listened to her speak of her village, the horses she had tended, her father, the days she and her sister had spent together as children. When she yawned, looking sleepy, Lask rose and walked with her back to her tent.

"Oh dear," Myranda said as they approached her tent, "I've gone and talked all about myself and haven't asked a thing about you."

"Just as well," Lask said, as if to himself. To her curious look, he continued, "I like hearing about you."

"It couldn't have been very interesting."

"To the contrary," Lask replied, "You fascinate me." Indeed, listening to her talk had been a most welcome distraction from the otherwise heavy thoughts that would have occupied his mind.

Myranda looked up at him and reached out to take his hand saying,

"You've been very kind to me, probably more than anyone has ever been. Thank you."

"You are most welcome."

Myranda stepped forward then and wrapped her arms around him. Lask was a bit surprised at first, but welcomed her to him, enveloping her in his tall form. Myranda smiled and leaned her head against his chest for a moment, finding his embrace was strong and warm, making it difficult to leave. At length she drew back and drifted away from him.

"Goodnight, Myranda," he said, as she parted the canvas of her tent, and a part of him smiled inwardly at how reluctant she seemed to answer,

"Goodnight."

Chapter Twenty

When Lask awoke, he knew it was very late. Not entirely sure why he was awake, he lay there for a moment, then sat up. He got to his feet and drew his cloak around his shoulders, slipping his feet into his boots to wander outside.

The camp was quiet and the fires burned low. He wandered along the perimeter for a time, seeing that all was quiet, then decided to see if Myranda rested. When he reached her tent, he slipped one finger through the door, raising it just enough to glance inside. Part of him hoped she was awake, while another part hoped that she was at last getting some sleep.

What he heard was distressed gasping, an uneven intake of breath and the restless shifting of blankets. Concerned, he slipped inside, whispering,

"Myranda?"

She did not answer. By the thin moonlight from outside, he could see her there, huddled on her side amid the knotted blankets, struggling against something he couldn't see. She was dreaming, tears staining her face, clutching at the blanket with a low whine like a frightened animal. Lask knelt to lay a hand on her shoulder, saying,

"Myranda."

She cried out and curled herself tighter, trying to escape whatever attacker tormented her in her sleep. Lask ran his hand along her shoulder, down her arm, calling her out of her nightmare,

"Myranda."

Her eyes snapped open with a gasp and her gaze darted around for a moment until it settled on the one who knelt at her side.

"Lask," she whispered. She said nothing more, but her tortured eyes spoke as though she had screamed at him.

He reached out and drew her to him, feeling her bury her sweat-beaded face against his neck. He rubbed a hand along her back, saying,

"You're safe now. The horrors of our dreams cannot follow us here."

"Mine did," she answered, voice hushed and hoarse. She released him, settling back, but still kept a hold on his hand. "Thank you."

Her hand was cold, so Lask shed his cloak and draped it over her as an extra blanket, murmuring,

"Go back to sleep. You are safe here."

He planted a foot to stand up, but Myranda gripped his hand tighter.

"Stay," she whispered. "Please. At least until I am asleep."

Lask obliged, sitting down on the tent floor beside her, letting her keep a hold on his hand. She held it against her face and he stroked a thumb over her cheek.

"Tell me about your homeland," whispered Myranda. "What is it like there?"

"Beautiful beyond measure," Lask replied with a fond smile. "Etheria is like a jewel; emerald fields and sapphire skies and waters that sparkle like diamonds. In the south are golden plains that dance like an ocean in the wind, and in the north are great mountains, ancient spires that crest into the heavens. I live in the middle kingdom, among the forest. There the trees are as old as the world, towering into the sky, a cathedral grown out of the land itself. Their leaves are lush and green, and as it grows colder, their edges begin to turn gold. They do not fall like the ones here do, but turn golden in the chill, gilding their branches by the first snowfall. There are no dead leaves on the ground, only soft grass that feels like silk under your feet. In all the years of my life, I have never grown tired of walking among those trees." He paused, seeing that she had drifted off again and gently freed his hand of her grip. "And perhaps one day you shall see them and walk beside me there."

Chapter Twenty-One

Myranda awoke to the sounds of the soldiers stirring outside and found herself curled up under the warmth of soft black fabric. The memory of the previous night came back to her as she hunkered there under the folds of Lask's cloak. He had appeared out of the darkness to her in the midst of her nightmare, pulling her back into the safety of his embrace.

Myranda wrapped her hands in his cloak, drawing it tighter about her. The fabric carried his smell; that crisp, masculine scent of him, reminiscent of rain, that made her smile. Reluctant to leave the cloak's warmth, she made herself get up and set about getting dressed.

As she was doing so, Lask was already up and making his way through the camp. He sent out the scouting parties for the day, then approached Myranda's tent, calling,

"Myranda?"

"Yes?"

Lask parted the flap to look inside. She had covered herself with his cloak when he called, only half dressed, but she didn't seem to mind.

"Just a moment and you can have this back," she told him.

Lask let the flap drop closed, the image of her bare, silken shoulders fresh in his mind. It wasn't long before Myranda emerged, reaching up to pin his cloak around him.

"Other side," Lask said, guiding her hands over to his other shoulder.

"Over your left?" she asked, "Your right arm will be covered."

"Left-handed," Lask explained.

Myranda was a bit surprised, but noticed too that his sword was strapped so that it could be drawn with his left hand. She decided she had been too distracted by his other unusual characteristics to have noticed. She fastened the pin, then smoothed the wrinkles out of the fabric at his shoulders.

"Thank you," she said. "It helped."

"I'm glad." He considered her with a slight, fond smile. Realizing his eyes were lingering longer than they should have, he cleared his throat saying, "We'll be setting out soon. I'll send someone to help with your tent."

Myranda smiled to herself as he swept away.

Chapter Twenty-Two

Galator had flown straight up into the clouds to escape the howls and barks that sounded below as the guardians of the Gate chased after him. He had been taking stock of the Gate's defenses, estimating the soldiers there, when he had been spotted. He cursed the horrid mortal trees and their lack of foliage.

Instead of banking to soar back up to the caverns in the north, he circled back and tucked his wings, landing down in the forest to creep back in on foot. He crouched low to the ground, prowling from shadow to shadow, until he heard movement up ahead and curled himself into a hollow of gnarled fir tree roots.

"Gone," came a voice and the griffin squinted through the darkness, sharp eyes picking out a tall wolf-like shape. Another was close behind.

"Fildahorr's not going to be happy we lost him," said the first.

"We can't help it he took to the skies and that the soldiers are lousy shots in the dark," protested the other.

Galator smirked to himself, watching the two warauls pad off into the forest back toward the Gate. Dawn was not far off, so Galator curled himself up tighter among the tree roots, tucking his head back under his wing to rest for a time, but did not fully sleep. As the sun was rising, he caught the sound of shifting leaves. His ears perked, hearing the sound coming closer. Peering around the trunk of the tree, he could see a waraul walking alongside a human on horseback.

The griffin dug his claws into the tree, scaling the trunk to conceal himself in the needles before they passed by his hiding place.

"They are not far," the soldier was saying, "We should reach the road by noon. Just wait at the edge of the forest and I will tell them you are here."

"Good," said Fildahorr. "As much as I do not want to relay this news, he ought to know."

Galator waited until the pair had passed out of earshot, then opened his wings, flapping up into the cold morning air. The forest spread out below him in all directions as far as he could see. The pair below had a long walk ahead of them. Galator soared high, heading west, flying for perhaps an hour until he came to the edge of the forest and spotted the road far below that ran along the edge of the woods. He followed it southward until his keen eyes spotted movement in the distance.

A small army, one far too familiar, traveled there far below. Galator looked them over, estimating at most five hundred soldiers. The griffin thought back to what he had overheard, and knew the pair had been heading out to make contact with Lask. The griffin spotted the commander there at the head of the column. Perhaps he would be foolish enough to venture into the forest alone. Galator decided to wait, gliding high above them in the cloud cover, unwilling to pass up such an opportunity.

Chapter Twenty-Three

That afternoon, while Lask and his soldiers were on the road, the messenger Verdin came riding out of the woods in the distance, approaching his commander and general. When he rode up beside them, he said,

"Sirs, Fildahorr is nearby with news."

Lask nodded and glanced back over his shoulder.

"Anarra," he said, "You and Horace lead them on and start setting up camp. Forge and I will catch up to you."

Anarra nodded and Lask turned his horse to follow Verdin off the road, Forge guiding his mare along behind them. The messenger led them across the field and into the privacy of the forest. Once there, a creature emerged out of the trees.

He resembled a large wolf, with tall spikes of fur that crested his head and continued down his back. He had large ears that pricked forward at the sight of them and intelligent brown eyes. There was something majestic in the way he held his head, a pride in his confident steps.

"Fildahorr," Lask said.

"Somadar," the creature replied with a respectful nod. "Galator was seen last night near the Gate. He was alone; no army accompanied him. We believe he was attempting to spy on us, and I fear he may have gotten a good look at our numbers before he was spotted."

"Did he make any attempt to pass through?"

"No. I imagine he did not want to risk flying over so many armed soldiers to get to the Gate. No doubt your soldiers could have shot him if he had. We pursued him on the ground as far as we could, but he soon flew too high into the night for us to see him."

"Which way did he fly?"

"Southeast," answered Fildahorr, "Heading back your way, perhaps to have a look at your numbers as well."

"Trying to decide how many mortals he will need to gather, I'd wager," Lask remarked.

"There have been several... *incidents*, sir," Fildahorr continued. "I'm afraid with all the comings and goings of the search parties it is getting harder and harder to remain undetected. They have done a good job of covering their tracks, but the nearest villages on the outskirts of the forest are growing suspicious. Twice people have wandered too near for comfort, and yesterday, one of the parties did not cover their trail well enough. We apprehended the man and he refused to keep quiet, so…" he paused. "Well, yesterday we were forced to do what I prefer not to." He glanced to Lask with a heavy look and the commander understood.

"You and your warauls have always had to do what you must to keep the Gate secret," he said. "While I would prefer you to avoid it as well, there are times it must be done."

"Ecthallia has accompanied one of the search parties north," said the waraul, letting the matter go. "They believe they may have found a good trail. She asked me to send the message along to you. She will await you at the ruins of Daeyi to relay whatever information she finds."

"Good," Lask said. "Thank you, Fildahorr. Let me know if your warauls catch sight of Galator again."

"Of course, sir."

The waraul nodded and he and Verdin disappeared back into the forest, leaving Lask and Forge alone.

"I don't like the idea of having Galator watching us," Forge said, as the two turned to head back out of the woods.

"I imagine he has been for a while, and every chance he gets," Lask replied. "After all, he can fly high enough to avoid detection and his eyes are keen."

"Still," Forge muttered. He paused, then asked, "Do you hear something?"

They fell silent, and Lask caught it as well: a high whistle, accompanied by a low, whooshing vibration, like rushing wind. A shadow passed over the sun and Lask looked up just in time to see the shape dropping out of the sky.

The griffin fell between the pair in a blur of rushing feathers. He kicked his hind legs out into the belly of Forge's horse, sending the mare toppling over, and battering Theramancer with his whipping wings.

Lask's horse reared up and Galator lunged at him, Theramancer jumping away to go streaking back into the forest. Lask's sword was out in an instant, sweeping up to deflect the claws that came swiping at his head. He let Theramancer run where he would. Galator was whizzing through the trees all around, his great wings propelling him forward to catch up to the galloping stallion. The griffin swerved and banked, ducking around the trees and weaving over and under the low hanging branches. With a bird-like shriek, he caught up to the horse and Lask whipped his sword back to deflect the snapping beak as Galator dropped down over him.

The griffin swooped up out of reach, only to dive again as they charged through a small clearing. Lask let go of the reins, letting Theramancer choose their path, and locked his feet in the stirrups to stand and meet the griffin. Galator dropped again and Lask swung his sword around, knocking the claws away and slicing down the length of the griffin's arm. Galator screeched and swooped up, disappearing among the leaves, but Lask knew he wasn't gone.

Just then, the griffin plummeted out of the trees behind him, throwing himself forward at Lask's head. Lask ducked and the griffin went hurtling over him and his horse. Galator tucked his wings, throwing himself back in a loop to dive down again, but Lask was ready this time. He blocked the claws, spinning his sword around to slice down the griffin's side. Instead of falling back like Lask had expected, Galator pushed ahead and Lask held his claws back with the flat of his sword, struggling against Galator's strength, the griffin's beak snapping inches from his face. Theramancer let out a shrill nicker as the griffin's back claws grazed his flank. Mustering his strength, Lask heaved the creature back, freeing his sword to crack the griffin in the head with its pommel.

Galator recoiled, wings flailing, and fell behind. Lask looked over his shoulder, trying to keep the griffin in his sight, but his horse carried him over a rise and Galator was lost amid the woods. A shadow passed over the forest floor and Lask was sure the griffin still followed him. Reaching down, he took the reins, pulling his horse into a slower pace. He came to a halt, looking up into the trees, but he could see nothing for the thick evergreen foliage. He stood ready, bracing himself for the attack that was sure to come.

"What concern is this world of yours, Somadar?" came the inquiring voice of the griffin. "It is not this land you are bound by blood to save."

"If you are in it, it becomes my concern," Lask growled in reply. "Show yourself and let us finish this now. I will slay you as I should have done on the battlefield!"

A low chuckle rumbled from somewhere overhead.

A stick snapped and Lask whirled to face his attacker, but instead Galator came plummeting down on the other side. Lask swung his sword around, but the griffin rolled in the air, dodging the blade, and threw himself forward, his claws sinking into Lask's shoulder and his weight heaving Theramancer over into the leaves.

Lask could hardly see in the chaos. He could feel Theramancer floundering beneath him and he had to throw his weight over to avoid being crushed by his horse. The leaves were churned into a whirlwind by the stallion's flailing legs. Galator had fallen on top of him, his claws tearing out of Lask's shoulder and slicing down his arm. Lask managed to get his sword up and block the snapping beak, but one of the griffin's wings slapped him in the head, a bright flash of light exploding before his eyes.

On instinct, Lask swung out and was rewarded by a shrill cry from Galator. Just then, Theramancer kicked out, his powerful back hooves catching the griffin in the gut and throwing him back. The horse rolled upright and stood, pulling Lask with him. He clutched at the saddle horn, hot blood flowing down his arm, and looked to see Galator lying in the leaves, bloody, sides heaving, the wind having been knocked out of him. Lask kicked his horse forward, thrusting his sword down to strike.

Galator threw himself over and scrambled to his feet, opening his wings. He leapt into the air before Lask could charge him again, crowing,

"My claws will not miss your heart the next time we meet, human!"

With that, the griffin launched himself up through the trees, fleeing into the safety of the sky.

Lask waited a long while to make sure he was gone. When Galator did not reappear, he sheathed his sword, looking down to see four deep puncture wounds in his left shoulder and four gashes running down his arm. The wounds throbbed, oozing blood that soaked his shirt and stained his skin. Theramancer neighed deep in his throat, turning his head back to look at him. Lask clapped an appreciative hand on his mount's neck, leaning over to inspect the horse's side. The griffin's claws had only nicked him, and Lask was sure that the scratches would be gone by the next morning. He turned to look back the way he had come and nudged his horse forward, following his trail back to find the road. Before he could get there, Forge found him, having been following his trail.

"Holy hell!" his friend exclaimed. "Are you alright?"

"I'll be fine," Lask grunted. "Are you?"

"Bruised from where my horse fell on me, but nothing a good night's sleep won't heal. Is Galator—?"

"Fled. The coward."

"Guess that answers the question of if he's been watching us," Forge muttered. "Come on, we'd best get you back to the camp."

Chapter Twenty-Four

When Lask and Forge arrived at their camp, Horace and Anarra came running.

"What happened?" asked Horace.

"You saw Galator?" Anarra said.

"Yes," Lask replied. "Or rather, he saw us."

"Shall I send for Salìt?" asked Anarra.

"No, I can take care of it," Lask answered. He hauled himself out of the saddle. "If you could see that my horse is tended."

"Of course, sir," replied the Serin leader, taking Theramancer's reins to lead the stallion away.

Lask trudged off toward his tent, Forge following him, asking,

"You're sure you don't want any help? That looks—"

"I'll do it," Lask said, voice a low growl through the pain in his shoulder.

The general conceded, leaving him alone.

Lask grabbed some bandages and a small bottle of wine from the supply carts and then entered his tent, letting slip a bit of the stoic mask he had worn as he walked through the camp. He unfastened the clasps of his shirt one-handed and winced as he slid it off. Looking down, he inspected the four punctures that pierced along his left shoulder, and the gashes that spread down from them. Sinking down, he grabbed a rag just as Myranda came barging in.

"Forge said you'd been hurt," she said and stopped short at the sight of him. "That's awful! You *do* need a healer—"

"I can take care of myself," Lask replied and uncorked the wine bottle.

"This is no time to be drinking!" Myranda exclaimed.

"It's not to *drink*," Lask growled back, as if it were obvious, and promptly dumped the wine over his shoulder. He stiffened and let out an almost animalistic snarl of pain. He noticed Myranda's shocked expression and said, "It will clean it better than water." Having let the wine sit for a moment, he took up the rag and began dabbing the blood away from his wound.

Myranda sank down beside him and took the rag from his hand, saying,

"I'll do it."

"I don't need—"

"You've got no business trying to wrap this yourself," Myranda shot back. "You told me that you are not my commander, therefore you can grouse all you like, but I'm not going anywhere."

Lask gave her a sour look from the corner of his eye, starting to regret those words. Nonetheless, he sat still and allowed her to clean his shoulder. As Myranda did so, she noticed the scar at the top of his left arm. It was a bird shape, and she realized she had seen it before. Glancing over to where his cloak lay discarded on the floor, she found the same shape on the pin there; the simple black hawk that was set over a golden, seven-rayed sun.

"One more scar for you," she remarked, looking back to his wounds.

"I doubt those will scar," Lask replied.

"These won't, but this one did?" Myranda asked, skeptical. She pointed to the pale grey lines of the hawk scar.

"That one was not properly tended while it was fresh," Lask replied.

"Was it intentional?" Myranda asked, curious.

"No."

Myranda waited to see if he would say more, for she was intrigued, but he offered no further explanation. Deciding not to bother him while he was in pain, she asked instead,

"Is there something you would like me to put on this?"

"Yes. In my bag there, you will find a jar. There is a poultice already prepared in it."

Myranda went and opened his bag, digging through his spare clothes for the jar. As she did so, she caught sight of the edge of a book under one of his shirts, a red leather cover with a few golden letters showing that read: *The Many Creatures*. Curious, but having no time to look at it further, she pushed it aside, finding the jar he had requested.

"Bring that little leather box as well," he said.

Myranda picked it up and carried it over to him, sitting back down beside him. She opened the jar, dipping her fingers in to dab a bit over his wounds. Lask yelped, shifting away on instinct.

"Oh don't be a baby," Myranda muttered, her hand following him.

"Then don't just jab at me," Lask grumbled in reply. He took up the leather container and pulled the top off. The seedling inside had grown two more leaves in the past days, so he didn't feel as guilty about plucking one. He slipped the tender leaf into his mouth, ignoring Myranda's doubtful look. Noticing the seedling was looking a little starved of sunlight, he leaned over to set it down in a patch of evening sunshine that was streaming through the tent door.

"Why are you carrying that around with you?" asked Myranda. "Gardening isn't exactly a very portable hobby."

"It is a tree from my homeland," Lask replied. "I found its seed in the bottom of my bag when I arrived here and planted it. Their kind are sacred and should be cared for."

"But it's alright to pull their leaves off and jostle them around in a saddlebag?"

"Their leaves have powerful healing properties," Lask replied, ignoring her accusations.

Myranda wrapped his shoulder, saying as she tied off the bandage,

"It's still early so it will likely be a while before supper. You should rest."

Lask looked over at her, unaccustomed to being given orders.

"You *should*," Myranda said, defensive under his scrutiny.

"I had planned to," he replied, shifting over to lay out on the blankets that had been laid down there.

"Would you like me to wake you for supper?" asked Myranda, rising.

"If you would, please."

Myranda nodded, then slipped out of his tent. She returned to her own tent for a time, unpacking a few of her things and deciding to see if she could manage a nap herself. Though she was never able to drift off, she lay there in the fading light that filtered through the canvas, listening to the sounds of the camp outside; the sounds of passing footsteps in the grass, the rattle of pots being unpacked to prepare supper, the cracking of wood as it was set up for fires. Someone was singing in the distance, though he was too far away for her to hear the words. She listened to the voices of the soldiers as they passed, catching snippets of their conversations.

"—don't like the idea that he's been watching us."

"I can't wait til we leave this godforsaken place. It's so dreary—"

"—wonder if there even *is* green here."

"So stale smelling. Have you noticed?"

"I do miss her, especially here…"

"They're so young. I just can't believe it—"

"I hate it here."

Myranda listened, wondering what was so bad about her kingdom that it had practically all of the soldiers complaining. Then again, if their homeland was as beautiful as Lask had described it, she decided she would have been homesick as well. At length, she thought it was probably nearing the time for supper, so got up and went back outside. She passed Forge, who was muttering curses into the cauldron he was stirring (probably because he'd burned something yet again), and went on down the row to Lask's tent.

She slipped inside, finding him asleep. She knelt there beside him, but he seemed to be resting so well, she was reluctant to wake him. Deciding that Forge hadn't finished cooking anyway, she settled down in the floor to wait a little longer. She glanced over at his bag that sat, still open, beside her.

Curiosity nagged at her, so Myranda slipped a hand in and pulled out the small red book. She opened the cover, seeing the words *The Many Creatures of Our Land, as researched and recorded by Faileas Sirodar*. The writing was elegant, a work of art in itself, and she knew it could have only been written by a renowned and well-practiced scribe. Turning the page, she skimmed over the table of contents:

Dragons, Fairies, Unicorns, Griffins, Centaurs, Hydras, Moranters, Warauls, Phoenixes, Drokamerdors, Merfolk, Humans—

Myranda paused, wondering why humans would be listed in a book of fantastical creatures, and so turned to the appropriate page to find out.

Humans were the first creatures to walk this land, the book told her, *The Great One placed into the world the seven First, who were charged with specific tasks to set up and govern the kingdom. This government, and the First's descendents, rule our kingdom to this day. I will discuss each of the First, in order of rank, below.*

Addicus was made the Réasdar, who was given the task to rule over all others in the land. It was through the Pact that

Addicus made with the Great One that magic was given to our world. The High Kings of our land have been descended of Addicus, down to our current High King, Lavancer.

Lu'corian was named the Somadar, charged with the duty of protecting our land from evil and harm. He put in place many of the defenses that still guard the King and our world. His sword and all of the duties that accompany it have been passed through his bloodline to the current Somadar, Lask.

Myranda stopped and looked over at the man who slept beside her, surprised. She had seen that Lask was obviously an important man, but according to this book, he was one of the most powerful men in his kingdom, second only to the king himself. Myranda glanced to his sword that lay nearby. It was an impressive weapon, with excellent craftsmanship. The grip was bound in black leather, the crossguard and pommel gleaming golden; gilded or some other gold-toned metal she did not know. Intricate vines twirled along the crossguard out to a flared wing shape at either end. Set into the pommel was an enormous emerald, bigger than any gemstone she'd ever heard about. As she considered it, she found herself wondering how old the weapon was, if it had indeed been passed through his family.

She heard Lask draw a breath from beside her and looked over to see his eyes blink open. He started a bit when he realized she was sitting next to him.

"Sorry," said Myranda. "I was going to wake you, but decided to wait another moment or two."

Lask's eyes glanced down to what she held in her hands and Myranda was startled at the sudden shift in his expression. Where he had looked glad to see her, his face darkened in an instant, like storm clouds blown in from the sea, eyes suddenly blazing. He sat up, demanding,

"What did you read?"

"Not much," Myranda answered, a bit frightened by the sudden, piercing edge on his voice. She snapped the book shut and handed it over, pinned down under those fierce eyes. Lask's hand curled around the book and drew it near to him, as if protecting a child.

"*What did you read?*" he growled.

"Just a few paragraphs," Myranda confessed, not daring to lie to him, "About the nobility in your kingdom."

"And that is all?"

"Yes. Whatever you are trying to hide, I didn't find it."

Lask's eyes cooled a bit and Myranda felt as though she had been released from a chokehold when his gaze at last turned away.

"I'm sorry," she said, "I didn't realize it was so important. I was just curious."

Lask cocked an eyebrow and glanced back to her.

"I do not let many people enter this tent," he said, "And those that do know well to keep clear of whatever may lie inside it." His face softened at her guilty expression, unable to be angry with her. "Since you did not look very far, no harm has been done." He reached over and tucked the book back into his bag before getting to his feet. "And now, I would imagine that our supper is ready."

Lask pulled on a clean shirt, favoring his injured shoulder, fingers working through the clasps as he strode out the door. Myranda followed him, glancing back to where he had stashed the book, wondering just what it was he guarded so closely.

Chapter Twenty-Five

Myranda's mind was working the entire time she ate, listening to Lask and Forge talk, glancing between them, the curiosity gnawing at her. She decided that since she had spent the previous evening talking about her, it was only fair for Lask to do the same. She made a resolution to try and work some answers out of him, so waited until Forge got up to go his own way for the evening, then looked over at Lask to ask,

"Why did you come here? You came after the griffin, I know, but why *you*?"

"Because it is my responsibility," Lask replied, not entirely sure what she meant. "I am sworn by blood and honor to defend my kingdom and keep order in it if needed. Galator is of my kingdom. I cannot simply leave him unleashed on yours." He noticed the way Myranda watched him, not sure what to make of the shrewd, keen expression she had fixed him with.

"Why did *he* come here?" she asked. "Did you not know what he would do?"

"He did not come here by our bidding," Lask replied. He saw just how curious, expectant she was, and so continued, "Galator led a rebellion in our kingdom. I was able to defeat him fairly soon after his initial uprising. His brother, the leader of the griffin race, came to me on the battlefield and begged me to spare his brother's life. Galator was chained and taken before our Senate and he was sent to live in exile under the guard of a very powerful individual. On the way there, he turned on his guards, fighting his way free, so that he could flee as far as he could imagine: here."

Myranda was silent for a moment, watching him with all the sharpness and leashed intensity of a serpent ready to strike.

"You let him live?" she said after a moment. "You had a chance to kill him and you let him *live*?"

"Galator's brother made a passionate plea on his behalf and traitors are often brought to trial. We had no idea that he would—"

"*Everything* I ever loved is *gone* because you could not do what *should* have been done!" Myranda snapped. "This creature, who rebelled against you and everything you are meant to protect, should *never* have been let to live another day. You held in your hand the life of a monster and were too weak to crush it!"

"Life is sacred and should not be idly—"

"Tell that to the damned beast who came and *slaughtered* everyone I knew!" Myranda shouted back. "No amount of idealistic thinking will change the evil that simmers in the hearts of some. My mother was shot in the back, my sister raped and murdered, and *you* could have stopped it with a single *word*!"

Myranda rose and stormed away from him, disappearing into the shadows beyond the fire's glow. Lask made no attempt to pursue her, for he knew he had no explanation that would satisfy her. Her world was a very different place from his. She did not know how Ossifer had begged, how Galator had agreed to live the rest of his life in servitude under the watchful eyes of an Ancient. In the end, he decided, it did not matter; she was right. For a moment, he had held Galator's life in his hand and he had not taken it. Lask turned his gaze into the fire, knowing he would never make the same mistake twice.

He thought back on the day. It had starting raining in the night, slicking the battlefield into a mess of mud, grass and blood. The two armies had struggled in the darkness, Lask leading a charge in from the side and driving the enemy back from the castle. The torches sputtered in the rain.

The Immortal

There was no moon. The lack of light made it hard to tell friend from foe and the second it took to figure it out could cost a man his life.

As the sky begin to lighten, shifting from churning blackness to sullen grey, Lask had managed to come face to face with Galator on the hill. The griffin had tried to flee and had been shot twice in the wing as he flew, making him resort to running across the wet grass. Lask had cut him off, standing between the griffin and the safety of the dense forest.

Claws sparked off of armor as the two flung themselves at one another, clawing, hacking, falling into the mud, scrambling up. Lask's sword found its mark easily on the exhausted griffin, drawing deep lines of crimson that ran like ink in the rain. Stabbed in the side, Galator whirled, only to have that terrible blade slice over the side of his face, just missing his eye. The griffin collapsed over into the bloody grass, gasping, too exhausted and weak to rise. Lask stepped close, stained with dirt and the blood of his enemy, and raised his sword up, ready to plunge it downward.

All of a sudden, a black shape dropped out of the sky, flinging itself between Lask and Galator. The dark griffin crouched over the fallen Galator, one hand raised, looking up the poised blade to Lask's face.

"Stand aside, Ossifer!" Lask growled.

"I beg of you, Somadar," cried the griffin, "Stay your hand. Spare his life."

"After what he has done?"

"My doing," Ossifer said, voice pained, "Our father's doing. We would not listen and he knew no better way to make himself heard. The blame is mine, lord—"

"Do not grovel, brother," snarled Galator from the ground. "I need neither your mercy nor his!"

"Please," said Ossifer, ignoring him, his golden-orange eyes never leaving Lask's face. "Try him as a traitor, imprison him, do what the Senate deems fit, but do not take his life. Do not deal him death as punishment for my sin. Allow him to live and I will try my best to undo what has been done." The griffin bowed his head down. "You hold the power of judgment, Somadar. I beg you act with judgment like our Creator's and be a man of mercy. Show my brother the grace that was never shown to him by me. Let him live as a prisoner if you must, but let him *live*."

Lask looked out over the battlefield, seeing his soldiers routing the last of Galator's army, claiming victory. He stood there, looking down his blade, still stained with the blood of his enemy. Ossifer knelt there in the bloody grass, head bowed, wings dragging the ground and covering his brother's wounded form, in such a pose of shame it seemed obscene for so magnificent a creature. Lask lowered his blade.

"You," he called to the nearest soldiers, "Bring chains to bind him. We will take him to the castle." Turning back to the griffins before him he said, "Galator, you are hereby captured for crimes of high treason, sedition and murder. For this you will be bound in the castle dungeon until the time you are brought before the Senate to answer for your crimes, after which you will be submitted to whatever punishments are due you."

"Thank you, Somadar," whispered Ossifer, bowing his head to the ground at Lask's feet.

Galator just lay there, wheezing on the grass, glaring up at him through a bloodied emerald eye. If only Lask had known what would grow from the simmering rage in those eyes, then he would not be sitting here in the mortal kingdoms.

He was sorry for what had happened to Myranda, and thought that she had every right to be angry with him. In her place, he likely would have felt the same. Still, there was some part of him that recoiled at the thought of having her hate him. He glanced toward the shadows where she had disappeared, as if willing her to return.

Lask shook his head. It was foolish. He had known her only a few days; there was no reason she should have so much pull on his emotions. Yet somehow she did and that fact sent his mind grappling with itself. She was a mortal, but a fraction of his age, ignorant of all the things that had shaped his existence. Somehow though, Lask thought that there was something in her eyes, a keenness in the way she looked at him, as if she understood all that he was without needing to know. She was one of the few people who did not recoil at the first sight of him, certainly the only mortal he had met who did not. She was not afraid of him. Indeed, Lask found the way she had consistently held her ground before him very attractive. He shook his head again. It was of little consequence now. She would blame him for the tragedy that befell her and would hate him for it. He doubted there would be anything he could do to change that.

To his surprise, some time later, Myranda reappeared out of the darkness and came to take a seat beside him again. Lask glanced over at her, not knowing what to say, or if he should say anything at all.

"I'm sorry for shouting at you," Myranda muttered.

She sighed, then looked over at him. Lask was taken aback when he saw no trace of hatred in her face. Frustration was there, certainly, and pain, but no longer anger and no trace of malice.

"You're a good man," she said, "And it is because the world is not half as good that terrible things come to happen. I can't seem to find it in myself to blame you for that," she looked over at him with a wry smile, "As I much as I might like to."

"Thank you," Lask replied. He looked back into the fire with a slight, relieved, smile. "I do try very hard to do the best thing, but for all my trying, I still lack the gift of prophecy. Had I any idea what would come of mercy, I would never have given it."

"Well," Myranda said after a moment, "You keep telling me that everything happens for a reason." She leaned over and wrapped her arms around his neck and Lask heard her voice by his ear. "Let's hope you're right."

He felt the soft brush of her lips on his cheek and then she was gone, releasing him from the warmth of her embrace. Lask looked after her as she left and felt the cold chill of the night air take her place around him.

Chapter Twenty-Six

Brogen had not stood a chance. An older, portly fellow on his way back from visiting his sister, he was passing through the woods that morning alone. Still bleary-eyed from sleep and drink, he did not feel the eyes upon him.

Galator sat in the top of the tree behind him, still and silent as if he were a branch himself. The griffin was hungry and needed to send a message. He waited until he had a clear shot through the trees, then spread his wings and dropped onto the unfortunate man.

Brogen didn't see what hit him. He felt something large plow into him from behind, knocking him over with the force, amidst a rush of wind that scattered the leaves. Iron-hard talons dug into his back and he struggled free of them with a shriek. He thrashed in the mud and the leaves, fighting himself free of the beast. He heard a squawk and looked over his shoulder to see a fierce monster behind him.

The griffin leapt after him as he ran, claws slashing down his back. Brogen ran as fast as his knobby legs would carry him, looking back to see Galator right behind him. The man's foot snagged on a tree root, sending him toppling, rolling down into a gully and Galator, seeing his prey cornered, leapt down after him.

Chapter Twenty-Seven

Biran rode at the head of the small scouting party, leading the way beside the Etherian scout Maresyn. Asbern and Sifkin rode behind, answering questions from the other scouts, along with Fusco, though he was too busy eyeing a female soldier by the name of Cerae.

"I've never seen a lady soldier until now," Fusco remarked, "I quite like it."

"Sounds like you've got an admirer back there," teased Maresyn from the front.

Cerae rolled her eyes and tried to ignore the mortal.

"Do you fight like a man?" asked Fusco, "Or are there other things that lady soldiers do?"

"Shall I show you?" growled Cerae, hand on her sword.

"Easy, love," said Maresyn, with a facetious smile.

"Love?" Fusco echoed. He looked between Cerae and Maresyn. "Oh, you're—"

"Married," Cerae growled. "For *quite* some time."

"Right," said Fusco, with a guilty smile. He glanced up to Maresyn. "Sorry, mate."

Sifkin rolled his eyes, embarrassed for his brother, but Maresyn just chuckled.

Without warning, a shrill scream echoed out of the woods up ahead. Viran's horse snorted, startled. Maresyn urged his horse on in the direction of the sound and the others followed. The scream came again, the voice breaking.

As the scouting party crested a hill, they looked down into a gully to see a flared pair of tawny wings. An unfortunate man floundered under the griffin's claws, blood-soaked and torn. Galator's head swung back over his shoulder, spotting the scouts.

Cerae's bow was raised and nocked in an instant, but Galator sunk his claws into the screaming man, launching himself into the air, sending the arrow clattering off the rocks.

"After him!" shouted Maresyn.

Galator was flapping above the treetops, carrying his victim like an osprey with a fish. The scouts wove through the trees, chasing after him. They did not dare take another shot upwards, for fear of hitting the man that hung beneath him. The griffin banked, turning a sharp about-face in the air and took off back the way they had come, wings pumping him higher and higher into the air. The scouts turned back after him, but the griffin had disappeared among the clouds.

Chapter Twenty-Eight

Lask and his soldiers had traveled through the morning and into the afternoon. Lask was just asking Horace about the terrain up ahead when he caught sight of a shape in the road.

"What is that?" asked Forge, shading his eyes against the sun to peer into the distance.

As they drew nearer, there was a disgusted cry from somewhere in the ranks.

It was a body. An older man lay on his back in the road, torn and raked with long slashes. Partially eaten, intestines lay spilled into the dirt beside him, blood outlining his shape like some gruesome halo. He lay there in the dust, eyes wide and mouth gaping in an expression of horror up at the sky.

"Dear God," breathed Horace.

Lask could tell the body was several hours old, but still he scanned the trees beside the road and looked to the sky, making sure that a dark shadow did not lurk above them.

Forge was doing the same, but neither saw any sign of the griffin, whose grim work lay before them. Myranda sat there on her horse beside Lask, a hand drawn up to her mouth, eyes wide.

"We can't just leave him here," said Trasiel.

"You and Astikin hold back," Lask replied, "Tend the body with whatever rites are customary of your people. I will leave a few soldiers to guard you in your task." He motioned to a few of the soldiers in the ranks behind them.

As the few separated themselves to hang back, the rest of the army passed on, giving a wide berth to the victim.

"Galator's work," Forge said as they continued on. "Means he's been lurking around again. We must be getting nearer to his hiding place, if he's resorting to trying to scare us away."

Lask nodded, having thought the same. He called a halt earlier than usual in a place Horace had chosen for them. Lask sent out a few riders to locate the nearest scouting parties, to find out if anyone had seen the griffin that day. Sure enough, it was not long before Maresyn and Viran's party came riding in, having already been heading back to report.

"Sir!" said Maresyn, pulling his horse to a halt. "We came upon Galator attacking a man. We tried to save him, but the griffin took to the skies."

"We found his victim in the road," Lask replied. "How far off were you?"

"Twenty miles, perhaps a bit more, to the northwest."

"Only about thirty miles from the coast," Viran added

Lask nodded and dismissed the scouts, noticing that the mortals looked shaken. He left orders for the scouts to concentrate their efforts in the north, reminding them once more to shoot the griffin on sight if they came across him. Having done so, Lask walked through the camp toward his tent when he spotted Myranda.

She looked up at him, still looking shocked and upset from the sight of the body, so Lask reached out and pulled her to him, enveloping her in his arms. Myranda wrapped her arms around his neck and tucked her face in against his chest. Though he was cool, she could feel a faint warmth through his shirt, a contrast to the cold evening air. She lingered there, not wanting to let him go, for she felt very safe there against him, as if nothing in the world could hurt her, a security she had not felt in a long time.

Lask did not mind having her there, clutching him to her. She was very warm, and he could feel her body relax a bit as he held her, settling into his embrace. At length, she whispered,

"Thank you."

"You are safe here," Lask promised her.

She looked up at him, and Lask studied her, seeing the way she looked at him; unafraid, both strong and vulnerable, not needing his affection, but craving it, beseeching him with her gaze to accept her, inviting him nearer. Lask suddenly felt very at home with her arms around him, as if he had discovered the place he had been searching for and not known it, and before he could even grasp what he was doing, he bowed his head to brush his lips against hers.

Like the river at last flowing home to the sea, they came together. Myranda leaned against him, pressing her lips against his in return, wrapping her fingers in his hair to keep him there. Lask's hand trailed down to the small of her back, drawing her in tight against him, reveling in the sweetness of her kiss. The wind was cold on their backs, but the warmth that blossomed between them kept them oblivious to its chill.

Myranda pulled back and blushed, although she could not hide the guilty smile that had crept onto her face. Lask smiled at the look, keeping her there against him. Not one for flights of romantic fancy, he could hardly believe he had indeed kissed a woman he had known only four days. As he felt Myranda tuck her head into the crook of his neck, he found he had no qualms with the idea and thought he would gladly do it again.

The two of them lingered by fire that night as they had done before, talking about nothing in particular and Lask noticed Myranda shifted herself over as they spoke until she was close enough to lean her head against his shoulder. As soon as she had done so, she raised her head again suddenly, saying,

"Your shoulder! How is it?"

"It's fine," Lask replied.

"It's only been a day, it couldn't possibly be *fine*. Here, let me have a look at it."

She reached for the collar of his shirt, fumbling the clasps loose. One side of Lask's mind shouted at him to stop her, but the other side didn't particularly care and was enjoying her touch, so was able to keep him uncertain long enough for Myranda to open his shirt and slide it down off his shoulder. She gasped.

Where there had been deep bleeding wounds the day before, there were only a few faint lines on his skin, smooth and fading.

"Told you it was fine," Lask said, glancing over to gauge her reaction.

"How...? How can that be?" asked Myranda, voice hushed. She looked at him, studying his face and her eyes locked with his gaze. Though he looked anxious, his eyes still beset her with that eerie chill, an infinite coldness that made her feel tiny sitting there under his gaze. "What are you?" she breathed.

"What do you mean?" Lask asked, voice quiet, afraid to break the tension that had suddenly snapped taut between them.

"Your eyes," said Myranda, "They are so different and strange—"

"Obviously—"

"I don't mean the color," she whispered, never turning from his gaze. "There is something endless about them, as though they have seen more than anyone could imagine. When you look at me, I feel as though I am in the shadow of something great and fearsome. There is a coldness about them, a chill I have felt before, when I laid beneath the griffin's stare. That sameness frightens me."

"There's no need to be afraid—"

"What *are* you?" she whispered again.

Lask looked away from her then, turning his eyes into the fire. He wanted to tell her, but he was afraid to, afraid of what she would think and do, worried that she might tell others. In the end, he replied,

"I am old."

"How old?" asked Myranda, both desperate and terrified to know.

"Seven hundred and ninety four." His words resonated like a bell in the stillness.

Myranda drew back from him, shaking her head.

"You can't be," she said, "You'd have to be—"

"Immortal," Lask finished.

Myranda watched him, wary, studying his face, which remained turned toward the fire. Things began to fall into place in her mind, the fragments melding together into a monolith of revelation in her mind.

"How?" she asked.

"I was born that way, as were all of my people."

Myranda was silent. Lask watched her face, unable to read the veiled expression there. He wanted to reach out and touch her, but he was afraid she would recoil from him, and so remained still. He had never thought about his Immortality very much, as it was commonplace in Etheria. Even on Earth, he had not dwelled on it, just accepting the fact that he was surrounded by mortals who could not know and could not understand. Now though, after seeing the wariness and fear that had settled into Myranda's eyes, he felt like a monster and as he thought about it, he realized that she had every reason to fear him, yet he could not live with having her look on him in fear.

"Why did you kiss me?" she asked at length.

Lask was taken aback, not having expected that question out of all the other possible responses she could have made.

"You can't love a mortal," she continued. "You would only watch me wither and die. So was I just a diversion for you while you were here?"

"No," Lask replied, "Of course not. There are ways that mortals and Immortals can be together—"

"You'll not give up your immortality for me," Myranda growled.

"No," Lask replied with a slight smile. "I'm not sure I could even if I wanted to. There are ways for us to be together, and I hope that you will simply trust me on that for now."

Myranda eyed him, wariness dissolving into curiosity. She reached out and touched a hand to his face, trailing her fingers over the curve of his cheek and along the line of his jaw. Lask sat perfectly still, afraid the slightest movement might scare her away. Her fingers traced down his throat and onto his collarbone, still bared from where she had inspected his wounds. Her fingers followed the lines of the healed gashes, expression fascinated. She looked back up to his face, meeting his eyes, then leaned her head in to brush a soft kiss over his lips. When she pulled back she said,

"I suppose it doesn't really matter how old you are or where you come from. You are the kindest man I've known and I respect and like you a great deal. That's all I really care about in the end."

Lask smiled, surprised and relieved at how accepting she had turned out to be. He reached out, brushing a bit of her hair back behind her ear, holding a new admiration for the woman before him.

There was a sound from nearby and Lask looked up to see the Letian healer, Yothan, step from the shadows, holding a bow, arrow nocked and drawn back tight.

"I knew there was something wrong with you," the man growled stalking in closer. "I could see the Devil in you. Abomination!"

Lask rose, slowly, hands raised, finding a center of balance with his footing, knowing it would be difficult to catch the shot at such close range.

"Hey!" came a yell from one of the soldiers nearby, seeing what was happening.

"Stop this!" shouted Myranda, moving for Yothan.

"Myranda, don't," Lask growled.

In the instant before the soldiers reached him and in the split second Lask's gaze turned to the side, Yothan let go.

Lask collapsed backward as his soldiers tackled the healer, wrenching the bow from his hands. Myranda screamed. Forge came running from around the corner. Lask clutched at the arrow embedded in his chest, gasping, too shocked to feel the pain. He felt Forge grab him by the shoulders, propping him up, saying,

"Shit!"

Myranda stood by, horrified, at a loss.

"You!" shouted Forge, pointing at the nearest soldier, "Get his legs."

They hefted Lask up between them, carrying him away to his tent while the others bound Yothan up like a caught calf. Myranda trailed behind Forge, following them inside, watching them lay Lask out on the blankets.

"Pull it out," Lask snarled.

"I should—"

"*Pull it out now.*"

Forge hesitated, then set his jaw, getting a grip at the base of the shaft. With one swift yank, he wrenched the arrow free of his friend's chest. Lask let out a harsh roar, arching with the agony.

"Get Salit!" Forge snapped to the soldier, Drake.

"No," Lask growled before the man could leave. "It's too late for that." He lay there, gasping, bringing a hand up, fingers instantly drenched in crimson.

"Don't just stand there!" yelped Myranda. "Help him!"

Lask looked over to her, catching her gaze. Myranda was struck by the steadiness in his eyes.

"It will be alright," he whispered to her.

"In theory," Forge muttered.

Lask shot a look at him, then tilted his head back, wincing. He closed his eyes and his breath shuddered, then ceased to come at all.

A crushing silence descended over the tent and Myranda brought trembling hands up to her mouth, looking on, disbelieving.

"Start praying, Drake," Forge growled at the soldier who stood by, looking lost and horrified.

Myranda's shaking breath was drowned out by the wind that was picking up outside. It whipped stronger and stronger, howling through the trees in the distance, flinging open the tent door. Myranda looked over her shoulder, out into the night, to see something glowing on the horizon. It came nearer, a wisp of golden fog swept in on the shrieking wind. It wound through the camp, soldiers stepping out of the way, shocked. The mist curled into the tent, casting its golden light over a stunned Myranda, an awed Drake, and an impatient Forge, then descended over the still form of Lask. It spread along his body, lapping like fire, following his shape, then sank into him, its light covered by the confines of flesh.

The wind died outside as quickly as it had come, leaving in its wake an eerie and desolate silence. For a moment, no one dared to move or even breathe, then all of a sudden, Lask drew a great breath, body arcing with the force of life, and he let out several hacking coughs before settling back and bringing a hand to his head with a grimace.

"Oh thank God," gasped Drake.

"You bastard," Forge growled, glaring at his friend, "Don't you ever do that again." He clapped a hand on Lask's shoulder. "Alright there?"

"All things considered," Lask muttered.

Forge sighed and squeezed his shoulder.

"You'd better rest," the general said. "In the meantime, I'm going to see what to do with the man who murdered you."

Forge rose and left the tent, taking Drake with him. Myranda lingered, still standing off to the side, stunned and silent. Still panting a bit, Lask looked over at her.

"Sorry you had to see that," he said.

Myranda went and knelt down beside him, reaching out to his chest. There was a blood-soaked hole in his shirt, but not a single mark on his white skin. Myranda withdrew her hand, eyes roving over him from head to toe.

"You just *died*," she said, as if to herself. She looked up to his face, still flabbergasted. "What was it like?"

"The arrow hurt like hell. Thankfully death itself wasn't so bad."

"You've never died before?"

"Can't say that I have," Lask remarked.

"Then how did you know you'd come back?"

"I was hoping all of our sources were correct," he said. Seeing that it was not an adequate enough explanation for her, he continued, "When we die in our world, it is permanent. Here, it is different. If were are a killed by a mortal, then we will heal and come back."

"By a mortal?" Myranda echoed, catching on, "But an Immortal—?"

"Can still kill us here, just as a mortal can kill us in our own world," Lask finished. "Don't ask me why," he said to her confused look, "I don't pretend to understand the workings of magic."

Myranda decided not to pester him for more information and instead took to running a hand over his head.

"Please don't make a habit of that," she said. "I'm getting so attached to you, you see."

Lask smiled and reached over to take her hand, pulling it over to press against his lips.

"Believe me, I'm just as glad it happened as you are," he said. "I cannot afford to leave my kingdom, not in a time like this and I have no heir nor prospect of one at present, much to the Senate's disapproval."

Myranda didn't have any idea how the Immortals' government worked or how an heir would be determined, but she decided that Lask was too honorable a man to be pursuing her here if he had left a wife behind. Deciding it was not the time to ask about it anyway, she put the matter from her mind. She lingered for a moment, not wanting to leave him after what had happened, but nonetheless decided to let him sleep.

"I'm glad you're alright," she said, then leaned down and kissed him.

Lask looked after her as she left, almost wishing she would return. He lay there for a moment after she had gone, then sat up, pulling off his bloody shirt, not bothering to fish out a clean one. He cleaned the blood off of himself, then lay back out on the blankets, but did not sleep (one did not easily relax after being killed). He reached over into his bag and pulled out *The Many Creatures of Our Land*, flipping through it. He did not read any of the words, but rather just looked over the illustrations. They were exquisitely done, in vibrant colors, many adorned with gold foil or burnishing. His eyes wandered over the numerous creatures drawn there, over the trees and mountains, the vine knotwork borders along the outer margin of each page.

Lask found himself terribly homesick in that moment. He would not be relying on guides in Etheria. There, he knew the land, could walk parts of it in total darkness. There, he would have had whatever resources needed to track down Galator. He could have asked the dragon Scoarin to help them, or even Ossifer, but he could not risk them being seen here. He did not have to hide in Etheria. There, he was greeted with salutes and thrown flower petals, not splattering tomatoes. No one would have dared to take a shot at him in his own camp.

He lay there for a while with the book in his hands until there was the soft shifting of canvas and he looked up to see Forge peer inside. Seeing his friend still awake, the general slipped inside, coming to sit down beside him.

"This is bad, Lask," he admitted. "Everybody in the camp saw that gold fog. I'm sure the mortals have a decent guess about what happened. Yothan is a raving lunatic. We can't let him go. He will tell everyone who will listen and we'll have a rabble coming after us in no time. He *murdered* you right here in our own camp. We can't very well just look that over because you came back."

Lask looked up to the ceiling, thinking. There was really only one option, and despite it all, Lask was reluctant. Had Yothan been an Etherian, he would have been an infant, so young was he compared to the Immortals. In Etheria, Lask would have had the man locked away in the dungeon until he could be tried before the Senate, but he found himself in a far more savage time and place. He sighed and said,

"Kill him."

Forge nodded, having already known what Lask would have to do.

"How do you want it done?" asked the general.

"Have Salìt mix him a lethal dose of aphoras."

"We will have to force it down his throat."

"Then do it." Lask looked over at him with eyes hardened by necessity.

"I'll see to it then."

Chapter Twenty-Nine

"Did you see it?" asked Fusco of his brother.

"I think everybody saw it," Sifkin replied.

"What do you reckon it was?"

"It was him," Trasiel said, wrapping his arms around himself to ward off the chill, whether from the cold or the knowledge of what had happened, he did not know. "Yothan *shot* him. He should be dead."

"Something tells me he's not," murmured Astikin.

"We all knew something was different about them," Horace remarked, quiet, as if afraid to be overheard. "Tonight, I think we've learned just what it is."

"What do you suppose they'll do to Yothan?" asked Asbern.

"Kill him, I imagine," said Astikin. "What else can they do? It's obvious they don't want word about what they are getting out."

"Well now *we* know," said Fusco, "So—"

"We *think* we know," Horace clarified. "And if we are right, then we would be wise to keep it to ourselves."

The group nodded in unspoken agreement.

"Still," said Sorek, "Yothan is one of us. Can we really sit by and let these people kill him?"

"Do *you* want to go argue with his red-eyed majesty?" scoffed Fusco. "Something tells me you wouldn't get far."

"We could let him go," Sorek continued. "Sneak him out in the middle of the night."

"And leave him free to go wandering off, raving about what he saw?" asked Horace.

"What loyalty do we have to these people, these *monsters*?" hissed Sorek, voice low. "It's because of them Daeyi was burned to the ground. Yothan is one of our own, he should come first."

"He's a murderer," Jerryn protested. "Even if he were among his own countrymen, he'd likely be killed for it."

"We can argue all we like, lads," said Astikin, "But something tells me it's not going to make any difference." He nodded over to the side.

They all looked to see the general Forge walking alongside a slender, dark-haired man, who was swirling a mixture around in the bottom of a bottle.

"What do you reckon—?"

"Astikin and I will find out," said Horace, cutting off Asbern's question.

The captain and lieutenant rose, following the direction the general and the other man had gone. They came to the place where Yothan had been bound to a stake, sitting under guard. He saw Horace and Astikin approach and looked to them with wide, fearful eyes, though could not call out to them for the gag in his mouth.

"Excuse us, sir," said Horace, stepping up beside Forge. "My fellows and I were wondering what is to become of our companion."

Forge looked over to him and the captain had a hard time reading the general's face.

"Your fellow assaulted and gravely wounded our unarmed commander within our own camp," Forge replied. "By doing so, he has forfeited his life."

The dark-haired man had knelt before Yothan and was pulling the gag out of his mouth. As soon as he did so, Yothan started shouting,

"Run, Horace! It's too late for me! They're immortal! All of them! I heard the Devil say it himself! Abominations of nature! He'll lead you to your death! Don't trust them, don't—"

"Hold his head, please," said the dark-haired man.

The soldiers that guarded him grabbed onto Yothan's head, yanking it back and forcing his mouth open.

"Have mercy on him, sir," Astikin said to Forge. "Let us keep him prisoner til all this is over."

"I'm afraid it's much too late for that," Forge replied. He turned to them. "I am sorry. I hope you know that what I do, I do for the sake of my kingdom. I may not have the Protector's blood that flows in my commander's veins, but I am no less loyal to my kingdom's safety." He looked back to Salìt. "Do it."

Salìt nodded and uncorked the bottle he carried, pouring its contents down Yothan's throat. The man struggled, twisting in the ropes, trying to spit, but the soldiers held his mouth and nose shut until he was forced to swallow.

"It will be painless," Forge told Horace and Astikin.

The two mortals stood by, unable to find anything more to say, watching as Yothan sat there, looking horrified and angry. His eyelids began to droop, heavy as though with sleep, until at last his head lolled against his chest, looking as calm as if he were taking an afternoon nap. Salìt pressed a hand in against the man's neck for a moment, then looked back to Forge and nodded.

Horace and Astikin walked back in a heavy silence to where the others sat. When the two rounded the corner, they were surprised to see Lask sitting in the midst of the mortal soldiers, who were watching him with a mixture of looks, ranging from awe to anger to pure terror. He looked up when Horace and Astikin appeared and motioned them to have a seat.

"I have had one of your fellows executed this night," said Lask, "And I believe you have a right to know why. I am not a cruel man, nor a tyrant. I did not wish to slay your companion, yet he left me with little choice. You know, I am sure, that he shot me and I was fatally wounded. As I am sitting here among you, you will know too that something must have happened—"

"The fog," said Viran.

"My returning soul," Lask replied, "And the magic accompanying it."

"At least it proves you've got one," muttered Fusco. As if realizing he had, in fact, spoken aloud, he said, "Sorry, sir."

Lask, however, smiled.

"The magic you witnessed," he continued, "Was the magic of Immortality, the reason I am still here. If you have not already pieced things together: I and all of these soldiers accompanying me are immortal, as is the creature we pursue. No one in your kingdoms can slay him, hence why we are here. As such, we wish to keep our presence relatively secret. We do not want to be hindered in our effort to catch the griffin, nor do we want mortals attempting to locate our homeland. Believe me, it would only end badly for you and we do not mean you any harm. Had I allowed Yothan to go free, he would only pose a continued threat to me, my soldiers, and our home. I had not wanted the truth of this matter revealed in such a sudden manner, but circumstance will not allow otherwise. For the time being, I ask that you keep this among yourselves. I would prefer not to take any more lives on secrecy's account."

Chapter Thirty

When Lask went out of his tent in the morning, he found Forge lingering nearby waiting for him.

"We'll be meeting Ecthallia today, on the far side of the ruins of Daeyi. We'll probably be there by noon or a bit after," said the general. He paused. "Perhaps you'll want to prepare Myranda for it."

Lask looked away in the direction of Myranda's tent. There was no going around the village, though he knew it would be torturous for Myranda to return there.

"I don't mean to sound rude, brother," said Forge, voice quiet and careful, "But what exactly are you doing there?"

"What do you mean?"

"With her." Forge nodded in the direction of Myranda's tent. "You've known her a matter of days and already you've kissed her and look at her like a swooning pup. Everyone can see it. The soldiers are talking. I've even heard a few remarks about you paying her favors for some, ah... distraction. It's not sitting well. If word gets back to Etheria, and you know it will, the Senate is not going to look kindly on your taking a mortal mistress."

"I'm not," Lask growled.

"I trust you, I do," Forge said, "But I've never seen you like this about a woman, no one has. She's a mortal and a commoner, at that. What in the world, Lask?"

Lask sighed.

"It's her, Forge."

"What do you mean?" He shook his head not understanding.

"From that night Navar sent me into the forest, the woman I saw. It's her."

Forge's brow furrowed into a skeptical scowl in the direction of Myranda's tent.

"I would know her anywhere," Lask said, voice quiet. "Her face has haunted my dreams for centuries."

"You are sure?"

"Yes."

Forge was silent for a moment and Lask murmured,

"I cannot lose her, Forge."

His friend looked at him and nodded.

"Alright," he said. "If you're sure, then you know I will be behind you always. Damn the Senate and damn the gossip then. If she's the one, then you must do what you have to."

Lask smiled.

"She is a fine lady," Forge remarked.

"She is indeed," Lask admitted. He sighed, remembering the task at hand. "I hate to ask her to go back to that dark place." He paused to considered the idea. "I will ride at the back today with her. You will lead everyone on. She may need a moment to linger and I will stay with her for that. I don't think being a little late to meet with Ecthallia will make too much difference."

"Fair enough," said Forge. "Though you do remember what happened the last time you were off by yourself?"

"I should only hope Galator is stupid enough to try his hand with me while Myranda is so close."

Forge chuckled, knowing well just how dangerous Lask could be when protecting the people he loved. Lask left him to oversee the preparations for departure and went to approach Myranda's tent. She was coming out just as he walked up and she smiled at him with such warmth, so happy to see him, Lask felt terrible about what he was going to have to tell her. Seeing his expression, her smile faded and she asked,

"What's wrong?"

"I'm sure, being a native of this land, you know where we are," Lask said.

"Yes."

"We must go through Daeyi today," he said, as if a confession, deciding not to talk around the issue. "With what happened, it has become a desolate and avoided place, one of the few where an army the size of our combined forces can remain undetected. I am meeting my lieutenant and her soldiers there, perhaps half a mile on the other side of the village."

"We have to go through it?" Myranda said, voice quiet.

"I'm afraid so."

She looked lost and terrified of the prospect. Lask put his hands on her shoulders saying,

"I have already told Forge that you and I will ride behind everyone else and arrive at the camp later if need be. If you find you need time, I will stay and watch over you."

Myranda reached out and took his hand, squeezing it.

"Thank you," she whispered.

"I am sorry I must ask this of you," said Lask.

Myranda held his hand against her face and murmured,

"Me too."

She held his hand there for a moment, then kissed the base of his palm and released him, turning to disappear back into her tent. Lask looked after her, wanting to followed, but stopping himself, and his mind drifted to the night so long ago when he had first seen her.

Pale moonlight had dappled the black forest floor as he crept through the shadows. Faint pinpoints of light danced in the air and all the world was crackling in the peak of its magic. So many things had already appeared to him in the darkness; horses and banquets and visions of death. It was the Night of Illusions and the world was churning.

"Go out into the night," the dragon had said, "For the world knows your place in it and it shall tell you. Listen well, for all your future lies written in the hand of the world's magic."

Lask trusted Navar and knew the dragon was following him in the air far above out of sight, but Navar had told him it was only a precaution. Navar could not see the illusions that Lask would, so unless the dragon spotted real danger, Lask was on his own in the face of the night's magic.

The young man tried to keep his sense about him, but the forest was eerie that night, and he could feel the magic creeping along his skin, prickling his spine, and in the darkness it wasn't long until every sound seemed like a threat. His own quickened breath seemed loud in the silent air, and he could hear his heart thumping in his ears as he walked deeper and deeper into the Carthonian, where the trees were almost as old as the world.

There was a shape up ahead and Lask froze. In the shadows, a large, sinuous feline shape unfurled itself before him and came to stand in the pool of moonlight opposite him. It was an enormous golden lion, haughty and fearsome. Its mane rippled along its neck and shoulders and it flexed iron claws into the black soil. Lask stood very still. He had no weapon, for Navar had said no good would come of carrying one this night. He was wholly vulnerable before the golden beast, and the lion seemed to know it.

It circled him, watching, calculating, and Lask turned in place, never taking his eyes from it. The lion snarled at him and feinted a swipe with its paw, but the young man did not flinch. The wind stirred and the trees seemed to whisper, "Hypanthon, hypanthon... the banner, the banner..." The lion seemed to hear the sound too and let out an outraged roar. Sheer instinct made Lask take a step back and as soon he moved, the lion threw itself forward.

Lask crossed his arms over his face as it lunged for him. The lion plowed him over into the grass and Lask grabbed onto its jaws to keep them from snapping over his face. He kicked his foot up into the creature's gut and the lion roared, straining against his hands to bite him. Lask wrestled its head to the side and kicked at it again, managing to struggle free. He took off at a sprint and could hear the lion charging after him, its harsh roars ringing off the trees.

There was a light ahead of him, and Lask ran for it. The light molded itself into a pale green moth, glittering magic wisping off its wings as it flew. Lask did not know why, but he began to chase it, running like a fleeing stag through the forest as the lion came streaking after him. The moth led him around the trees and Lask followed, leaping over streams and brambles as the lion panted at his heels. The moth fluttered, impossibly fast, through the night and just as Lask burst into a clearing, he heard the lion roar to lunge.

He braced himself, expecting the creature to come crashing into his back, but all that hit him was a blast of hot wind, tangling his hair, whipping in his shirt, and then it was gone. Lask stood, panting in the sudden stillness and lowered his arms that he had brought up to cover his head. The night was quiet once again, stirred only by the perfumed wind.

Something glittered in the center of the clearing, and Lask realized there was a man standing there, clad all in white that shimmered as if it were embroidered with spider silk. His skin and hair were equally pale, as if the moonlight had become flesh in him. The only color he had was in his eyes, bright and red as embers, reflections of the eyes of the young man who looked back at him. The phantom raised a hand and beckoned him closer.

Lask obeyed, unable to defy the resonating power of the spirit. The coldness of him wrapped around the young man's ankles, chilled his skin, and when the apparition spoke, his voice tolled like a bell,

"Pick it up."

Lask looked to the spirit's feet. It was the sword, the one Lask had taken from his fallen father the day Hydrellia burned, the one that had weighed on the back of the Somadar for thousands of years, the one forged by the hands of the spirit that stood before him.

"I can't," Lask replied, without thinking.

The spirit's eyes sparked with anger.

"Pick it up," the phantom growled.

Lask looked back to the sword. It seemed so large resting there on the moon-bathed grass, and he knew it was not real. He had left that sword safe in Navar's cave for the night.

"Do you know who I am?" the spirit asked.

"You are Lu`corian," Lask answered, "Somadar, second of the First, father of my father's father, made by the hand of the One Creator."

The spirit looked satisfied and inquired,

"Then why do you refuse me?"

Lask had no answer for him. He stood in silence, feeling as if he were a fish in the sight of a heron.

"My blood is your blood," Lu`corian told him, "And you are bound to this purpose as I was. I know you and what is in your heart. You dream of a simple life, of sunflower fields and stables full of fine horses. You dream of a common house with common tasks and quiet routine. This is not your fate. You are man neither simple nor common and you will not get what you want."

Lask was silent, but could feel himself bristling. The spirit gave a wry smile.

"You are just like your brother," chided Lu`corian, "Unwilling to take up the fate the world requires of you. Weak. Coward."

"I am nothing like him. It should have been *his*," Lask snapped.

"But it's *not*." The spirit's voice was sharp and cut through the young man before him. "It is yours and you will not take it because you are afraid, afraid of what will be asked of you, afraid of what you might find in yourself, and afraid of living a life above the comfortable mediocrity you have let yourself desire."

Lask was silent, glowering at the phantom.

"Pick it up," Lu`corian hissed at him.

"Is that what you want?" Lask snarled back. "Fine." He reached down and snatched up the sword from the ground. It was heavy and hurt his hands, but he clung on to it anyway. "You had no choice in the matter. I suppose you think I shouldn't either. I will carry this sword because there is no one else to, because someone has to look after the kingdom you made, because everyone expects me to, and I will do it well, but know that in a corner of my heart I shall always hate you for the blood that runs in my veins."

The spirit smiled a little, a gentle smile, and said to him,

"Ah, Lask, you are yet so young. You will grow into a fine Somadar, the greatest since the days when I walked the land, perhaps even greater than I." There was a touch of pride in the spirit's voice. "You will not get all you desire, but I promise you, child, though times will be dark and that sword will be so heavy it will crush the breath from you, you will be happy in the end."

Lask looked at him, bewildered, feeling very small. The wind blew through the trees, whispering things he did not understand. Lu`corian disappeared into the wind before his eyes and the sword in his hands was suddenly light and soft. Lask looked down and found that he did not hold a sword at all, but rather a long scarlet ribbon, sewn with pearls and delicate gold embroidery. He shook his head, perplexed, trying to remind himself it was all just a trick of the magic, that none of it was real.

There was a quiet laugh from the edge of the clearing. Lask looked up and just caught the shape of someone disappearing behind one of the trees. Curious in spite of himself, Lask walked over and looked behind the tree. There was no one there. Faint footsteps sounded behind him and Lask whirled, catching sight of bright red hair flashing in the moonlight before the shape was gone again. He went after it, following the sound of the footsteps and laughter. They wove around the trees, turning and turning, the shape staying behind him wherever he spun, in a kind of dance, until at last, Lask found himself with his back against the broad trunk of a tree and he came face to face with the most beautiful creature he had ever seen.

The moonlight shone around her fiery hair like a halo and it reflected in the deep blue of her eyes so that they glinted like jewels. Her lips looked as soft as rose petals beneath the faint spread of freckles that kissed the fair skin over her cheeks and the bridge of her nose. She was older than he was and smelled of lilies and sweet spice as she leaned closer to him. He stood there against the tree as she tilted her head up, pressing her lips against his. Lask drew a sharp breath as the feel of her kiss swept over him. It felt like drowning and waking up all at once. It made him hungry and frightened and soaring with joy. He felt her hands sliding down his arms until they found his hands. Her fingers wrapped in the elegant ribbon and she pulled back to whisper on his lips,

"May I have this?"

"Certainly, my lady," he whispered back, still swimming in the delight of her kiss.

She smiled up at him and twirled one end of it around her finger.

"You hold on to that end," she told him.

Lask obeyed and wrapped the other end around his ring finger like she had. She backed away from him, slowly, her eyes never leaving his. The ribbon drew out between them.

"I will find you," she told him as the ribbon drew tighter, "And you will find me." The ribbon stretched taught. "Wait for me."

"I shall," he said.

She smiled at him, a bright enchanting smile, and when he blinked, she disappeared, as if dissipated into the moonlight, and the ribbon with her. He looked down and saw a bright line of gold magic wrapped around his finger where the ribbon had been and it seemed to sink into his skin, disappearing into him, leaving his finger blazing with warmth that seemed to seep up his hand and arm and settle in his heart. He looked back into the clearing, into the moonlight, but the woman was gone. He did not know if she were real, or ever would be, but already he missed her.

Chapter Thirty-One

The ground was black, as though tainted by the death that had soaked it. Charred timbers jutted out of the ground like fractured bones, mere skeletons of the homes that had been there before. Myranda held her horse back, watching the soldiers continue on, unable to take a step inside the perimeter. Lask held back with her, reining Theramancer in at a distance, wanting to give her some space. She let the distance between her and the soldiers grow, watching them disappear into the ashes and fog like ghosts. When they had disappeared, she drew a trembling breath and at last let her horse walk forward.

It was almost like having double vision. Myranda found herself caught between the picture her mind told her should be there and the terrible blackened remains that her eyes saw. She could hear her horse's hooves thumping against the scorched earth, the fainter echo of

Theramancer's behind her. She pulled her horse to a stop, looking at the three blackened timbers that still stood from one of the buildings on the outskirts of town, the rest of the structure collapsed and burned away entirely.

"That was my house," said Myranda, voice quiet and hollow. "I didn't save a thing from it except the clothes on my back." She let her horse continue on further into the village, until she stopped again, dismounting to wander, as if lost, down the street. "I tripped on my mother's body here," she said, looking down at the ground, the echo of her own horrified scream resounding in her mind from that awful night. "And there," she said, pointing ahead, "That was where my sister..." The words caught in her throat. "My little sister..." She sank down to the ground and let out a choked sob.

Lask dismounted and walked over to where she wept there on the ground. He knelt down behind her, laying a hand on her back.

"I couldn't protect her," Myranda cried, "I couldn't get to her."

"It's not your fault," Lask murmured, running his hands along her shoulders.

"She was always the weaker one, such a timid thing, scared of mice and spiders. She was going to marry the chandler's son in just a few more weeks, once spring came." She broke off and sniffed, wiping at her eyes. Pointing back to a few charred beams she said, "That's where I was born, where my mother sewed me blankets and my father told me stories of battles he fought and legends of monsters. If only he'd known they were real." Myranda reached down to the ground where her tears fell, gathering the ashes and blackened dirt. She cupped it in her hands, the ashes crumbling under touch, as she wept, "This is my life..."

Lask wrapped an arm around her, as if sheltering her there with his form, and rested his head on her shoulder.

"This *was* your life," he said into her ear, "And as terrible as it was to see it wrenched away from you, you shall be given another; perhaps a future greater than anything you dreamed for yourself in the days of your youth. There is no life that exists without pain, but there is no pain in life without purpose. Though we cannot often know why such awful things happen to such good people, we must trust that all things happen to accomplish a much greater plan. If there is one thing I believe it is that our Creator shapes our lives in ways we cannot understand, but are no less full of promise. He can use the destroying of one path to create another, perhaps a better one, that you would not have known otherwise. Perhaps it will take time to find your way to that new path, but He will not leave you without it."

Lask turned his head to place a kiss against her neck and tightened his arm around her. Myranda reached up to clutch at his arm across her chest, feeling still the crushing desolation that pressed in on her from the black surroundings, but she was aware too that she did not kneel there alone. She could feel the cold, stale wind on her face, but the warm strength of Lask's body was pressed against her back, sheltering her there in the folds of his cloak, keeping her drawn back against him so that she could not crumble forward into the ashes.

When at last she stood, she did so without a word. She approached her horse and pulled herself back into the saddle, setting off out of the village at a canter. Lask followed, saying nothing more. When they reached the camp, Myranda disappeared among the tents, and Lask let her go.

He handed Theramancer off to one of the grooms, then started off through the camp. He found who he was looking for as he neared the center. She was a small, slender woman with sharp blue eyes and brown hair she wore tied up behind her head. There was an angular grace to her features and a keenness in her glace, like a sparrow surveying a garden of bugs. She was dressed in blue and carried a bow slung over her shoulder. She clapped a hand over her heart when Lask approached.

"Ecthallia," he said with a nod. "It is good to see you."

"Likewise, sir." She produced a map of the mortal kingdoms, unrolling it for his inspection. "We believe Galator has been hiding and gathering his forces here, in the caves on the ocean," she tapped an area on the coast,

"However, our scouts now say that his army seems to be on the move southward."

"South?" Lask echoed. "Toward the Gate?"

"No, sir. Back toward Letiana."

"Why would he send them there?" Lask wondered, brow furrowed.

"Don't know, sir, unless it's another diversion to draw us away from the Gate."

"How many did you leave at the Gate?"

"A full Serin. Asmodeus and the Moranters have come in from the surrounding forest to help as well. With them and the Warauls with us, about six hundred altogether there."

"Good. Then tomorrow we shall split up again. We can't travel together; that's much too large a force to keep relatively hidden. You and your Serin will head south and pursue Galator's army. I will continue on to the caves in search of Galator. Do we know how many soldiers he has been able to gather?"

"The scouts estimate somewhere between five and seven hundred, sir."

"Then you should make quick work of them if you must," said Lask. "Capperith continues to guard the Gate from the other side?"

"Yes, sir. He and three Serins are camped in the Carthonian nearby."

"Good." Lask nodded. "Then let us hope our information is correct so that this might be over soon."

Chapter Thirty-Two

When Lask entered his tent that night, he started when he noticed a figure curled up on the blankets.

"Sorry," came Myranda's voice.

Lask knelt beside her, running a hand over her hair.

"Can I stay?" she whispered. "I don't want to be by myself."

"Of course," Lask told her.

He bent down and kissed her head, then sat back to unpin his cloak and pull off his boots. When he had done so, he lay out on his back beside her and Myranda instantly curled up against him, resting her head on his chest. Lask wrapped an arm around her saying,

"I had been worried about you this afternoon. I thought about going after you, but thought you might need some time on your own."

"I wouldn't have minded if came looking for me," Myranda said, voice tenuous. "This is a worse pain than I could have ever imagined and there are times that I wish that I had been killed too."

Lask shifted onto his side to face her, saying,

"Never wish that. I know how much it hurts to survive when all that you love does not, but I know too that there is always a purpose for those who do."

Myranda shook her head, eyes maddened with grief, and she grabbed onto him, rolling over onto her back and hauling him over on top of her.

"Just make me forget," came her desperate whisper in his ear. "I don't want to think about it any more. Make me forget. *Please.*"

She arched against him and Lask felt her hook one of her legs around his. He drew back and looked down at her, feeling her warm, yielding body beneath him. Her full bosom rose up to him with each breath and though her face was marred by grief, she was still lovely in the fading light. Bending his head down, he placed a kiss on her forehead, then shifted free of her, easing himself over to lie beside her once more. Myranda covered her eyes with a hand and Lask curled himself around her, resting his head on her shoulder.

"Do you think I'm a whore?" she asked.

"No, I think you're distraught," Lask replied, and the low murmur of his voice in her ear gave Myranda a bit of comfort.

She ran a hand along his arm that wrapped around her waist, unable to stop the tear that escaped the corner of her eye. Lask felt it slide from her cheek and drip onto the point of his nose.

"When I was a boy," he said, holding her in close to him, "I lived in a river-town called Hydrellia. I lived there with my mother and father and Malachi, my elder brother. And though my brother picked on me terribly and my father was a distant and cruel man, I was happy there. My mother would take me out into the town with her and all the people there were kind to me. I was young; I did not know much about the war that was happening then, that a man called Vortearigan threatened to break the very core of the kingdom. I knew what war was, but it was a distant thought, one I never imagined very clearly or understood.

One day, my brother and I were out on the hill that overlooked the town and we saw soldiers coming out of the forest. We knew that they were not our father's and went running back into town. My father jerked me along through the streets, running me home to my mother, telling us to stay inside, while he and my brother went out to fight.

We could hear the chaos and the screaming outside. After a while, something was thrown through the front window and we began to smell smoke. My mother left me in the back room to try to put the fire out, but it only spread. I heard a crack and her scream and I left the room to see that she had been pinned under a beam that had fallen. I burned my hands trying to help her, but she died there.

I fled from the house and into the street and all around me people lay dying. I saw my father and saw the horse coming behind him. Vortearigan's sword pierced through his back and he fell there in the street. I should have run, but terror held me still. Vortearigan saw me and came down from his horse to walk over. There was no mistaking who I was and I thought surely he would kill me, but he did not. He dug his knife into my arm, marked me with the scar I still carry, but he let me live. I don't know why. Perhaps he could not kill a child, or perhaps he thought I'd give him a bit a sport when I was older. Either way, once he had cut me, he left me there.

I took my father's sword and fled into the forest after my brother, but he would not take me with him. He turned on me as I pursued him, threw his knife into my leg and fled, leaving me there alone."

"What did you do?" asked Myranda.

"I wandered among the trees, lost and forsaken, until I emerged farther upriver near the falls. There I was found by the one who would become my true father, whom I would love very much and who made me into the man I have become."

"Who was he?" Myranda inquired, curious, in spite of herself. She felt Lask smile a bit against her shoulder.

"He was a dragon."

Myranda shifted a bit to give him an incredulous look. Lask chuckled and released her, rolling over onto his back, turning his head to look at her.

"His name was Navar."

"A dragon," Myranda said, still not able to imagine it.

"Yes, among the finest of his kind," Lask answered, looking up at the tent ceiling with a slight smile. "He raised both me and Forge. That is why the two of us are as close as brothers."

Myranda turned onto her side, curling up against him again as he continued,

"I do know what it is like to watch your life burn before your eyes, but I know too just how many good things can eventually come after it."

Myranda tucked her head in against his chest, listening to the steady beat of his heart under her ear, lulled by the gentle rhythm of his breath. They lay in silence for a time, the darkness deepening around them until the faint glow of the moonrise glimmered through the canvas of the tent. Myranda was still and in the quiet, her mind returned to that dreadful night, as it did whenever she stayed too still. She expected the tears she had shed earlier to be renewed as the thoughts crossed her mind, but they were not. The ethereal peacefulness that clung to Lask's presence was contagious. Indeed, though she was filled with sorrow still, it was not the desperate, maddened desolation that had filled her before. She took a breath to comment on it and then it occurred to her that Lask was asleep. Myranda realized she must have been lying there much longer than she had thought, for the moon had risen and a pale sliver of its light stretched across her hand through a gap in the canvas.

She raised her head, propping herself up to look at him to find that the sliver of moonlight continued on, stretching across his face, casting his white skin in a striking silver sheen. Lask was a handsome man, despite his odd coloration. There was an elegance to his sharp features, a fierce grace, like befitted a bird of prey. Myranda ran a hand along his face, softly so not to wake him, admiring its snowy curves and contours. Her fingers trailed over his strong jaw and down his neck, undoing a few of the clasps on his shirt to slip her fingers under the fabric to rest against his skin.

"I don't deserve you," she whispered to him. "I am just a plain peasant woman. I cleaned up after horses, picked the dirt from their hooves. But you, you are older than my kingdom, and almost a king yourself, respected and feared and admired. I don't understand why you would even look at me, but I'm glad you do. When I would lie awake as a girl and dream about the man who would come and woo me, I never once thought of someone like you. I thought I would be happy with a simple fisherman, or maybe a blacksmith, and maybe I would have been. I never dreamed I would find myself in the midst of such wondrous and terrible things, and certainly not that I would find myself under the gaze of such a man as you." She kissed his shoulder and she felt his arm tighten around her. "I'm sorry, I didn't mean to wake you." She looked up to see him smile at her and said, "Or have you been eavesdropping on me?"

The guilty smile on his face was all the answer she needed. Myranda thought she ought to have been embarrassed, but found that she wasn't. She smiled back at him, reaching out to run her fingers through his dark hair, whispering,

"Can I tell you something?"

"Of course."

Myranda considered him for a moment, looking uncharacteristically shy all of a sudden, then said,

"I think I love you."

Lask sat up a little, reaching out to cup her face in his hand with a quiet smile.

"That's good," he murmured, "Because I think I love you too."

He tilted his head, drawing her nearer to kiss her and Myranda settled back down over him, sliding a hand around to the nape of his neck. When he drew back, he lay his head down, closing his eyes with such a contented smile, it was as if there were no war, no threat of battle or bloodshed.

"Five days," he sighed. "I have been searching for the woman I am to love for centuries." He opened his eyes again to look up at her. "And I know, after only five days, that you are she. I knew from the moment I saw you. I saw your face long ago, in visions of magic, and long have I waited to find you."

Myranda smiled, running a hand along his face. Lask turned his head into her touch, basking in the feel of her fingertips on his skin.

"Centuries," Myranda echoed. "I can't even imagine. How can things stay the same for so long?"

"Change is brought by unrest," Lask replied. "If people are happy and the kingdom is thriving, what need is there for change?"

"I don't see how something could be that perfect."

"It's not perfect. If it were, I wouldn't be here," Lask said with an ironic smile, "But this is the first war in several hundred years."

"There have been two wars in the thirty years I've been alive," said Myranda. "I just can't imagine how a kingdom can exist for so long with so few problems."

Lask smiled. He eased her off of him saying,

"Here, let me show you something." He sat up and reached over for the small leather container he had set out when there was still sunlight and brought it over to him.

"It's grown quite a bit these past few days," Myranda remarked at the sight of the seedling.

"More than I thought it would," replied Lask. "This is a Eurydicen tree," he explained, "The first kind of tree to ever grow in Etheria. All of them that grow today are descents of a single tree that was Created when our world was formed. It is from that first tree that the Spring of Life flows, the gift from the Great One that gives the land its Immortality. Each Eurydicen contains just a bit of the magic from that very first one." He plucked off one of the golden-edged leaves and offered it to her. "Try it."

Wary, but curious, Myranda let him slip the leaf into her mouth. The leaf was smooth and easy to swallow. As she did so, she could feel the same tingle of its taste spread through her body. It was like every sense was waking up, as if she were suddenly more aware of every sensation. The night was no longer dull monochrome, but a lush combination of deep blues, purple and silver. Looking back to Lask, she thought his hair resembled raven feathers, so many subtle colors seemed to catch in it. His eyes were brighter; even in the darkness she could tell they were so rich a red, they would shame a rose. The sound of the wind outside seemed fuller, almost an echoing sigh. Her skin gave a tingle of delight from the brush of Lask's fingers as he reached down to take her hand.

"There was a bruise on your wrist," he said, and she thought his voice sounded even richer. "I had noticed it."

Myranda looked down, only to see that her skin was now unmarked, the purple splotch gone as if it had never been there at all. She suddenly felt very small and awed, but very much alive. It was as if everything were new, as if she had been given a glimpse into the oldest secret of the world, as if she had stolen a taste of the forbidden fruit. Even as she sat there she could feel the sensation already beginning to fade.

"Do you feel like this all the time?" she whispered.

Lask leaned over to her, brushing a kiss across her lips, and murmured,

"Would it not be a perfect world?"

Chapter Thirty-Three

Galator sat out on the cliffs in the late watches of the night, looking back to his soldiers in the field, who were returning to the caverns below. He could feel them looking up at him and thought it felt good to be admired and feared.

Several years ago, he had begun gathering the first of his army, exchanging clandestine messages with other griffins and humans outside of the mountain. He had been reading one such message when another griffin had entered his chamber. Galator shoved the paper behind him as the golden griffin entered.

"What do you want, Messalo?" Galator growled.

"The Rekan has asked me to tell you that he would like you to go down to Denmahi. The spring festival will be in a few days and the Rekan was invited, but cannot attend."

Galator hissed and Messalo shrank back a bit.

"If you would rather not," said the gold griffin, "You'll have to take it up with him."

Galator leapt down from the rock ledge, fluffing his feathers out and raising his head up above Messalo's so to look down at him with dangerous green eyes. Galator went out into the corridor and followed it around to enter the large chamber that belonged to his brother. Ossifer was sprawled out on a long pillow up on a rock ledge sipping from a bottle of wine.

"I am not your messenger boy!" Galator growled. "Sending me down to some foppish human display? What do you take me for?"

"It will be a fine time," Ossifer replied, "Lots to eat, plenty to drink. The humans know a good time, for sure. I would go myself, but cannot—"

"Too busy getting fat and drunk!" Galator spat.

Ossifer raised his black head, looking down at him with tired eyes.

"I was going to send my son," he said, "But I thought perhaps you would like to go instead, get out of the mountains for a while, have a spot of fun for a change. God knows, brother, you need some."

"Is that your cure-all then? You think you can make up for all that you have done by offering me a day of drink?"

"There is very little, I have found, that can't be fixed with a good wine."

Galator snarled and Ossifer gave a satisfied smile, knowing his words would annoy his brother.

"Yes, taunt me," growled Galator, "Try to make me your puppet, send me to the things you can't be bothered to attend yourself, take what little dignity I have managed to retain. The day draws near, brother, when that haughty smirk will fade from your face. I have more on my side than you know and it is high time I called on them. I will make you see what you and our father have done. I will make the entire kingdom see."

Ossifer's eyes narrowed.

"Galator," he said, "I know full well how our father treated you, but that is no fault of mine—"

"You made no effort to stop him!"

"And what of all those times he sent us out to hunt and I would always catch the deer, but let you claim it as yours? What of the times when you broke something and I let him blame me? Or when I found those letters so long ago that you'd been sending to the humans in Farisdon, trying to marshal some sort of rebellion and I agreed not to tell him?"

"You were a fool," hissed Galator, "For thinking you could ever persuade me otherwise."

Ossifer's head drew back a bit, his tail twitching behind him.

"What have you done?" he asked, looking down to where his brother stood.

"Things are quiet," said Galator, "The kingdom sleeps while the king and his Somadar tighten their grip, too concerned with their power to look to the north." He clacked his beak. "Enjoy your final days as Rekan, brother, for I shall pull you down from your perch and into the dust as you have cast me!" He turned to storm out of the chamber.

"Don't be a fool, Galator!" Ossifer crowed. "Challenge me all you like, but if you think you shall shake the rulers of this kingdom, you are sorely mistaken! Raise so much as a single claw against the king and the Somadar shall stomp out your life like the pathetic little snake you are!"

Galator turned his face into the freezing wind, letting the chill chase the memory out of his mind. Perhaps his war had not been as successful as he'd hoped, but he had still proven that the kingdom could be challenged, had shown his brother he was a force to be reckoned with. It would be a long time before Ossifer could be sure of his power again and the shame of his failure to contain his brother would follow him for the rest of his life. Galator was able to take a little satisfaction out of that.

Chapter Thirty-Four

When Lask awoke in the morning he almost panicked. Something was crushing his throat, denying him breath. As he came fully awake, he realized what it was. Myranda lay sprawled on top of him, her arm draped across his neck. Lask gently shifted her over a bit, pulling her arm down to relieve his burning lungs, then lay still so not to wake her.

She rested well, curled up against him under his arm, snuggled up on his chest. He ran his fingers up her back, twisting them in her fiery hair. He could feel the warmth of her breath fan over his chest with each rhythmic exhalation and then realized there was a small puddle of drool under her head from where her mouth was open. Lask thought he ought to have been disgusted, yet for some reason it made him adore her all the more.

Myranda shifted against him, a contented smile curving over her face as she found herself warm and comfortable. She opened her eyes, at last realizing where she was. She heaved herself off of him, exclaiming,

"Oh! Oh, I'm sorry!"

"I don't mind," Lask replied with a chuckle, "It was—"

"Oh and I spit all over you!" Myranda blushed and scrubbed her drool off with her sleeve. She gave a flustered sigh and sat up.

Lask sat up behind her, running his hands down her arms and bowing his head to whisper in her ear,

"I really don't mind."

She felt him brush her hair to the side to kiss her neck, unable to stay flustered under his attention. She felt his arm slip around her, drawing her back and she complied, laying back out on the blankets. Lask settled down beside her, propping himself up to lean over her. Myranda smiled up at him, brushing his dark hair back out of his face and saying,

"Say it."

"What?"

"What I fussed at you for calling me when we first met."

He let out that low, rumbling chuckle that reminded her of a cat's purr.

"As you wish," he said, bowing his head down to her ear, "My lady."

Myranda smiled, wrapping her arms up around his neck and turning her head to kiss him. When he drew back, he shifted down, curling himself around her to rest his head on her chest, as if mirroring the way she had slept against him.

"I feel like I've known you for years," he told her. "I've never felt more at ease around anyone. I have confided in you many secrets and yet I do not fear for any of them. Indeed, I believe I would trust you with my life."

Myranda ran a hand over his head, smoothing down his hair and Lask closed his eyes under her touch. It was then that she realized the depth of his trust. She had been told his greatest secret and as he lay there she was struck by how vulnerable he looked. She traced a finger down his exposed white throat, letting her hand trail along his shoulder. To the Earth, he was ancient. He was powerful and otherworldly, yet he trusted her enough to lie completely relaxed and defenseless in her arms. Myranda knew this was an illusion, that even now he could have her pinned to the ground if he thought her a threat, that he could likely kill her with his bare hands, but for some reason that made him all the more intriguing. He reminded her of the sea; inviting and untamed, elegant and deadly, a power and mystery that eluded understanding.

"How can someone like you, who is so old and who has seen so much, love such a fleeting weak thing like me?" she murmured.

Lask looked up at her with those eyes she no longer thought strange.

"My dear, you are anything but weak," he said. He picked himself up a bit and kissed her throat before continuing, "Every day you amaze me that you are so strong, so sharp and full of life and beauty in such short years, how you can shine when your world is so dim. I love that spark in you. And I love you, too, because you are not afraid of me, because you can stand before me and not recoil in the least. It fascinates me that so young a rock can withstand this old tempest." He gave a fond smile.

"I've always been fond of the wind," replied Myranda, returning his smile.

"Besides," he said, "You do not know what I'm supposed to be; you know only what I am. You know nothing of the history and the expectations that weigh upon me every day. There is not a soul in all Etheria who does not see the sword before they see me. It is because you are not of that world you are able to see the man who carries that sword."

Myranda ran a hand down his face, studying him. Just then, there was a voice at the door.

"Commander!"

Lask drew back, reluctant.

"Commander!"

The tent door opened and Lask cast a sharp eye at the soldier there. Myranda blushed.

"Sorry, sir," the man said and quickly dropped the canvas back.

Myranda released him and Lask pushed himself up, refastening his shirt and pulling on his cloak and boots. Grabbing his sword, he stepped outside saying,

"What is it, soldier?"

"Sir, our scouts, they were attacked last night."

Lask was instantly off, walking through the camp toward the healers' tent asking,

"Where? How many?"

"Three survivors, sir: two of ours and the mortal, Viran. They were coming back from a westward path, said they ran into Galator and a small battalion."

Lask entered the long healers' tent and Salit approached, wiping blood from his hands on a rag.

"I've done what I can, sir," said the surgeon, "Our two should be healed up in a day or so. I'm not sure about the mortal. He was shot in the side and I treated it as best I could, though I don't know enough about their physiology to say how well he will recover."

Lask thanked him, clapping a hand on his shoulder as he passed and went to kneel down beside one of his soldiers who looked the least injured.

"What happened?" he asked of him.

"We had gone out toward the west, looking for tracks in the area that Galator was suspected to be," Maresyn replied, voice quiet and rough through the pain of his wounds. "We were on our way back when we ran into him and a small force as he was heading south, maybe fifty men. There were only fifteen of us, counting the two mortals, and the enemy knew exactly what to do. They did not shoot to kill, but aimed only to wound us. Once fallen, Galator went around and finished the job. We three, we were each shot and our horses spooked and took off. I suppose that's the only reason we're alive. I let my mount run for a while, then dismounted and let him go, hiding myself and trying to cover my tracks. Sure enough, I was pursued, but they followed the horse and not me. I was able to circle back and found Cerae, who had done a similar thing. We found Viran not far off and dragged him with us into a gully. I went back to cover our trail and we hid out there for an hour or so til we were sure the enemy had moved on. Took us all night to walk back. We did not dare go back for the others. The griffin made quick work of them anyway. The other mortal, Fusco, didn't stand a chance."

"You did well," Lask said, placing a hand on his shoulder. He glanced to the other soldier, Cerae, who lay sedated and to Viran, then rose, going out of the tent once more to find Forge.

"You heard, I assume?" Lask asked when he located him.

"Yes. I was looking for you. What do you want done?"

"Send a group of soldiers, around two score, back to retrieve the bodies. Look for tracks to see if Galator's force continued south. Use caution. I don't know if it was chance that our scouts ran into them or if they were looking for us."

Chapter Thirty-Five

Lask kept the army camped that day, deciding to give his soldiers time to retrieve their fallen comrades and for the reports to come in with news of Galator's whereabouts. When the soldiers returned later that afternoon, they reported that Galator seemed to have continued south and that it was likely just bad luck that the scouts had run into him.

Lask was sitting with Forge soon after their return. Myranda was approaching as he was saying,

"I don't know what to do with them. That many fires will be like a beacon. We can't draw that much attention."

"Well we can't just not give them the proper rites," said Forge.

Myranda realized they were talking about the fallen soldiers, and announced her presence by saying,

"Why not just bury them?"

Lask and Forge both looked at her with such horrified faces, Myranda might as well have suggested the bodies be made into soup.

"I don't mean just sling them in ditch," she said, defensive.

"We only bury small children," Lask replied in explanation, "And even then, they are always buried under one of the sacred trees. To bury an adult, and a faithful soldier at that, would be a great disrespect."

"We're only about two days from the Gate," said Forge. "Perhaps Salìt would be able to treat the bodies with something to keep them decent and we can send them with Ecthallia to be sent back to Etheria. Capperith can take care of it."

"That is the best option we have, I'm afraid," Lask agreed. "Tell Salìt to do what he can. We will part ways with Ecthallia in the morning."

Forge nodded and rose. Before Myranda could even take his place beside Lask, one of the mortal soldiers came stomping over, roaring,

"My brother! My brother is dead! You have killed him!"

Lask rose to meet the irate Sifkin, replying,

"It was not my hand that took his life—"

"You sent him out there! You split us up! I could have looked after him! You sent him out there towards that *thing*, knowing full well that it lurked there."

"I am sorry for Fusco's death," Lask told him, "It is never my intent to harm any soldier under my command."

"Let me go," growled Sifkin. "Do not ask me to stay here. Let me go, take his body, give him a proper burial. You have others who can guide you and your scouts are learning this place quick enough. You don't need me."

"Very well," Lask conceded. "Go, mourn and honor your brother as you wish."

Sifkin's eyes were icy and he gave a curt nod, then trudged off into the camp the way he had come. Lask glanced over to see Trasiel there nearby. The soldier came over to him.

"Let me go with him, sir," said Trasiel. "He will need help moving the body and digging the grave, and he shouldn't be left alone in a such a state. I can rejoin you, and maybe persuade him to as well, once he has calmed down a bit."

"Go," Lask agreed, "But take caution. Do not light a fire or draw attention to yourself. The griffin and his soldiers may yet be about. We will take the northwestern road. You can catch up to us there."

"Thank you, sir."

Trasiel nodded and went away after Sifkin.

Chapter Thirty-Six

After supper that evening, Lask and Myranda were walking along the perimeter of the camp together when Myranda started off into the field. Lask followed, unsure of where she was going. When he asked, she turned back to him to reply,

"Things have been much too serious today. Believe me, I know more than anybody that one should not go to bed feeling so heavy."

Lask regarded her, agreeing, but not knowing what she was planning. She put her fists up, saying,

"Come on. I almost got you once. It's high time I finished the job."

Lask cocked an eyebrow, unable to hold back a smile at her. He shook his head, but Myranda took a swing at him. He dodged and she could see that mischievous spark kindle in him as she provoked his fighting blood. He gave a crooked sort of grin and paced a slow circle around her, like a panther stalking its prey. Myranda followed him, ducking when he surged in at her, pushing his arm away to swing a return at him. Lask caught it and his hand came in, stopping short just before her head. Myranda flinched anyway, though she knew Lask would never strike her.

She sidestepped away, circling back around him, looking for an opening, but finding none. She ducked low as he came at her again, swinging back at him, only to have him pin her arm against his side. Myranda pulled against him without success and swung at him with her free arm, only to have him capture it against his other side.

"Well now," Lask said with satisfied smile. "It's a good thing I'm not your enemy."

In truth, Myranda didn't mind being pinned so tightly against him, but she wasn't about to let him win. She brought her heel down on his foot and Lask yelped, surprised, and Myranda was able to squirm free of him. She lunged at him, catching him around the waist and setting him off balance to tackle him onto the frosted ground. Lask groaned and Myranda's hand rested against his throat.

"Surrender?" she asked.

"Never," Lask growled. He winced again.

"What's the matter? I didn't hurt you that badly."

He shifted with a grunt and reached beneath him. With a tug, he produced a large (and very squashed) pinecone. Myranda looked guilty, but snickered in spite of herself.

"First you nearly break my foot, then you go and drop me on a damned prickly pinecone," Lask remarked. "Not the fairest of fights."

"You're immortal, you'll live," Myranda answered with a teasing smile. "Or maybe you just don't want to admit a girl got the best of you again."

He looked up at her and Myranda could see the mischief in him, but didn't realize what he was about to do until it was too late. Lask grabbed her and heaved her over, hands clamping around her wrists to hold her pinned down beneath him.

"And perhaps *you* do not want to admit you are overconfident in your victory," he teased.

Myranda struggled, but Lask just held her there, not hurting her, but resting enough of his weight on her to hold her still. Myranda looked up at him and for a moment she could see the fierce, strange creature that pinned her. Perhaps it was easy to forget among his kindness and polite manners that she had, in fact, taunted a formidable predator. Myranda found herself thinking that if she were a sane woman, she should be terrified to be alone under those scarlet eyes and the strong, pale form that held her trapped, wholly at his mercy, and that no woman in her right mind would dare provoke such a man.

Lask could see the shift in her expression, the playfulness giving way to something else and he realized that he would be an altogether frightening thing for a woman to find holding her down. He released her instantly, as if his hands had been burned. Before he could sit back, Myranda reached up to cup his face in her hand.

"Truce?" she asked.

Lask looked back to her and saw no fear in her face, just a sort of warm curiosity, soft and beguiling.

"I didn't mean to scare you," he murmured.

"Scare me?" Myranda scoffed. "You shall have to do a lot better than that if that's your aim."

Lask smiled and Myranda ran a hand down his face. He had a warm, handsome smile that made him far less threatening and more of an ordinary man than a fearsome immortal. Myranda wrapped her arms around his neck, drawing him down to her.

"I figure if you wanted to hurt me you've had ample chance to do it before now," she said into his ear. "I trust you."

"I would never hurt you," Lask told her, "Never would I lay a hand on you in anything other than love." He bent his head down and kissed her then pulled back, shifting over off of her.

Myranda propped herself up to see him laying there beside her, defenseless beneath her gaze as she had been beneath his. She reached out to trail her fingers down his vulnerable throat and over his chest with a fond smile. She felt a strange satisfaction at the way he seemed to abhor the thought of being frightening to her, willing to lie there for her inspection to prove himself harmless to her. Myranda reached down and took his hand, pulling him up with her, saying,

"Come on, it's getting dark."

They walked back into the camp and Lask felt the warmth of her hand, the strength of her grip, as they passed through the rows and he glanced down at her. She kept easy pace with his long stride, with her head up, seeming at ease beside him. They were approaching his tent and Myranda showed no sign of parting from him.

"Staying with me, are you?" Lask inquired.

"Well if you don't want me to," replied Myranda, making as if to saunter away.

Lask caught her with a smile, towing her into his tent with him. Myranda wrapped her arms around him, feeling small against his tall form as he enveloped her. He bowed his head and kissed her, then released her, going to light the lamp that sat on the low table in the corner. Myranda watched him, endlessly intrigued, wanting to know everything he had seen in his long life.

"Tell me about your family," she said. "Was your father the Protector like you?"

"Yes, although I should hope I make a better one than he did."

Myranda waited to see if he would say more, but he didn't, coming to sit across from her in silence.

"And your brother?" she inquired. "From what you said he doesn't seem like a very good man. What became of him?"

"He is a thief, a murderer, and One only knows what else."

"Is?" Myranda echoed. "I thought all of your family was dead."

"He might as well be," Lask muttered. To her curious expression he said, "He has been in exile for several centuries now, banished by my own hand, for the murder of our former king."

"Oh." Myranda decided perhaps his family had not been the best choice of discussion topics. She lay out on her stomach on the blankets and inquired, "And what of women? In almost eight hundred years, surely there have been many."

"There have not," Lask replied with a smile at her curious and eager grin. "I have courted but a few, and none with any lasting intention."

"Never been married?"

"No. Have you?"

"No." She watched him for a moment, then murmured, "Surely it is lonely to have lived eight centuries by yourself."

"Sometimes it has been," Lask confessed, "But then I have always been alone, so I don't know what it would be like otherwise." He ran a hand along her back and said, "I must write down some orders for tomorrow. Do you mind?"

"Of course not. Don't let me get in your way, commander," she replied with a smile.

Lask's hand trailed off of her as he shifted away, settling down beside the low table and reaching over into his bag. Pulling out a long box, he withdrew a quill and inkbottle, then unrolled a bit of paper. He glanced to where Myranda lay before dipping his quill in the ink. He had put off writing this letter, but knew that they were nearing dangerous territory and so could wait no longer.

To my officers, he wrote, *If you should read this, then I have either been captured or killed. If I have been captured, send Forge to locate me. Free me if you can, but do not bend to any request Galator may make. If it happens that I must be left to my fate for the good of the kingdom, do so without regret.*

If I have been killed, then times shall be very dark indeed. Bring Malachi back to Etheria and imprison him there. Though a criminal of the worst sort, he will hold the only Somadar blood left in the world and it must be guarded. Lavancer can decide what should be done with him in the long term. As I lack an heir, then it is my wish that my sword and power be passed to my general, Forge, until the noble bloodline can be continued. His devotion to our kingdom is no less than my own, and it is my belief that he will make a fine Protector in my stead.

Regardless of whether I have been slain or imprisoned, send for Capperith and the remaining Serins immediately. We cannot afford to waste any more time in our pursuit of Galator. Attack and defeat him as swiftly as you can. If secrecy can be preserved, then it is well, but if not, then so be it. Just be certain that the location of the Gate remains undiscovered by the mortal kingdoms.

He paused and glanced over, seeing Myranda dozing there on his pillow. He dipped his quill again and continued,

Also in the event of my death, please see that Myranda is escorted into Etheria. Offer her the Long Life if she will have it and see that she is well cared for. Treat her as though she were my widow, for though I have known her but a moment of my lifetime, she has kindled in me such a spark of love that I know it would have blazed in the years to come had I but lived to love her.

Blessings be with you all and may our Great Creator look down upon your victory.

Lask folded the letter and sealed it, then set it there on the table. He then pulled off his boots and unpinned his cloak from around his shoulders. With a quiet breath, he extinguished the lamp and went over to slide in beside Myranda, pulling the blankets up over them. She drew a breath, waking at the movement next to her. She shifted over to give him more space, turning onto her side so she could run a hand up his arm.

"I was dreaming," she murmured, fingers twining in the ends of his hair that had fallen over his shoulder.

"About what?" he inquired, raising his arm for her to slide under.

"I was in Daeyi, before it was ravaged, and my father was there and so were you. The two of you were talking."

"Did we like each other?"

"I think so. The strange part was that I was a girl, but you were the same as you are now." She paused. "Then again, I suppose you probably *did* look same when I was a girl, before I was born even. Old codger."

Lask could hear the teasing smile in her voice through the darkness and found a lock of her hair with his fingers to give it a playful tug. He heard her laugh, a sound as pleasant as any birdsong. He turned his head to brush a kiss upon her forehead.

"Myranda," he said.

"Hm?" she answered, thinking her name sounded particularly nice in his accent.

"When this is over, when there is no more war, would you consider accompanying me back to Etheria? I don't think my homecoming would be nearly as pleasant without my lady beside me."

"Yes, of course. I should very much like to see your homeland."

Chapter Thirty-Seven

Trasiel placed the last shovel of dirt onto the grave, while Sifkin stood by holding the torch, looking as though someone had beaten him.

"He was a good man," said Trasiel.

"Aye, the best brother I could have had," Sifkin replied with a sniff.

"If only there were more like him," Trasiel said, "Perhaps none of this would have happened."

Sifkin nodded.

"And perhaps," continued Trasiel, "There would be no need for any of this. I am truly sorry, my friend."

Sifkin looked up, not entirely sure what he was talking about. Trasiel turned his head away, bringing his fingers to his mouth to produce a shrill whistle. There was the sound of shifting leaves and heavy footsteps. An armed man emerged from the dark forest around them, and another.

"Trasiel," Sifkin hissed, watching as even more men appeared out of the darkness, "What have you done?"

"I chose a side," Trasiel replied, "The one that made me the best offer. I'm afraid it was not yours. I am sorry."

Sifkin just looked at him as the soldiers closed in around him, too stricken with grief and shock to fight back.

Chapter Thirty-Eight

The next morning, Lask had his soldiers on the move early. They parted ways with Ecthallia, each section of the army going their own way. Lask led his soldiers to the northwest, toward the caves where Galator was supposed to be. It was mid afternoon when a shadow passed over the ground. Lask looked skyward, but saw nothing.

"Bird?" asked Forge, but his voice was low, knowing that it had been too large to be a bird.

There was a shout from the back of the column and Lask turned in the saddle to look behind them, toward the east, seeing men charging out of the trees.

"READY!" he called. "About face!"

The soldiers turned with a unified echo of stomping feet and scraping metal as swords were drawn, and they stood ready, awaiting the enemy that was pouring out of the forest onto the road below.

"Archers!" Lask shouted, "Mind the skies. If you see the griffin, take your shot!"

The enemy was almost upon them and the first volley of the Etherians' arrows arced up, slowing the charge's progress, but not preventing it. The two sides met with a cacophony of roars and ringing metal.

As the soldiers who had been at the back now found themselves on the front lines, Lask held back a stamping Theramancer, looking around. He had fought Galator before, and knew the griffin rarely sent forth just one charge. Sure enough, he caught a faint glint off in the trees.

"To the right!" he shouted. "Archers! The trees!"

A volley was sent off into the woods and they were rewarded by a chorus of screams. The rest of the enemy army began rushing out of the trees, no longer bothering to conceal themselves.

Lask's soldiers dug their feet in, lowering swords and spears to meet the oncoming charge while their fellows at the back still grappled with their own enemies. Rather than hitting straight on, the enemy turned, concentrating themselves to plow straight into the middle of the assembled Etherians. In the ensuing chaos, the ranks were split clean through.

"Hold the line!" Forge was roaring.

The dust of the road turned muddy as the blood began to soak in. The wind was picking up, swirling dust and leaves, only adding to the chaos. Lask blinked away the flying debris, swinging his sword down on the enemy soldiers like a reaper through the wheat. Theramancer kicked and snapped, trampling any foe in his path, cutting a swath through the enemy ranks.

The battlefield was a mess of blood and grit, the wind whipping, bearing the glowing mists of souls, copper and silver, heralding the return of the Immortals killed on the battlefield. They did not come as often as Lask had expected and as he looked around, he could see his soldiers lying in the road, gasping and bleeding, terribly wounded, but not dead. Galator had been sure to teach his men the best ways to incapacitate an Immortal without killing him.

There were more enemy soldiers than Lask had expected. For each one he struck down, two more seemed rush in. He was hacking his way through the ranks alongside Forge and glanced back to find Myranda. She was swinging her spear down from the back of her horse, cracking heads with the pole, stabbing out with the point, wreaking absolute havoc, so Lask did not fear much for her. Indeed, he had to give a slight smile at the vengeance she was taking on the enemy.

He heard an agonized roar from beside him and looked to see Forge fall from the back of his horse, speared in the side. Lask hauled back on the reins, preventing Theramancer from charging further. He turned back, sword slicing through the man that was bending over his friend.

Lask leapt from the back of his horse and down into the chaos, blade sweeping in all directions, keeping the enemy at bay. He stood over Forge, who was grunting,

"I'll be fine. Don't get yourself killed over me—"

Lask lunged over him, stabbing his sword into another enemy. He wrenched his blade free and looked out over the battlefield. His soldiers were slicing through the mortals, driving them back toward the trees. That was when Lask looked back toward the northwest.

Galator was flying in low, each wingbeat brushing over the brittle grass, and behind him came a new pack of soldiers.

Lask swung about, cutting down the pair of men who were rushing in at him, then looked back up. His ranks had already been broken once, and a fair number lay wounded. Galator and his men were not charging at the main body of Etherian soldiers, but rather aiming straight for the front, and Lask realized exactly what they meant to do. He knelt at Forge's side.

"You still have the letter?" he asked.

"Yes," Forge grunted. "Why—?"

"Whatever he asks of you, do not do it. You had better heal fast. Etheria is going to need you."

"What's—?"

Lask stood and pulled himself back into the saddle, deflecting the spear point that was thrusting in at him.

"RETREAT!" he roared over the melee. "FALL BACK!"

Galator and his men pierced through the front of the column as the main force began to withdraw. The enemy swept forward, cutting Lask off from the rest of his soldiers. He plunged into his attackers, blade slicing through, keeping them back, but not for long.

The enemy had left the Etherian soldiers, circling in around their commander instead, driving him back. They braved that fatal blade, pressing around his kicking horse, hands reaching up at him from all sides.

Myranda had been following the other soldiers as they withdrew, and she looked back, seeing Lask down below, encircled by his enemies, lashing out at them like a cornered beast. Myranda hefted her spear, turning her horse, but a hand grabbed the reins. It was Anarra.

"No!" said the Serin leader. "We must go! There is nothing any of us can do for him now! We have been too far divided and wounded. If Galator wanted him dead he would have already done it."

Myranda looked back, seeing Lask hacking at the hands that grabbed for him, Theramancer tossing his head, snapping and shrieking. Lask looked up then, as if drawn by her gaze, and he found her there on the hill. His voice rang up to her,

"GO, MY LADY!"

Myranda felt Anarra pulling her away, looking on in horror as Lask was hauled from the back of his horse and lost beneath his enemies.

Chapter Thirty-Nine

Galator's soldiers were unconcerned with the battered Etherian force, not pursuing them as the Etherians retreated back up the road, but regrouping in a field to the south. Anarra, the last unwounded officer, was shouting,

"Set up camp! Those unharmed will return for the wounded! Salìt!"

"Here, madam!" shouted the surgeon. Though tousled and blood-spattered, the healer had done a fair job of holding his own in the fight.

"Do what you have to in order to tend the wounded. You act with a Serin leader's power for the next day!"

Myranda walked among the soldiers, dazed. She left her horse in the hands of one of the grooms, and went to set up her tent, feeling lost. All around her soldiers were running, dragging men and women covered in blood. There was shouting and screaming, and the agonized cries of the wounded.

Chapter Forty

The ranks parted to allow Galator passage up beside his fallen enemy. The griffin stood there, staring down at Lask, who lay looking dead in the creature's shadow. Galator sat back on his haunches, reaching out to unbuckle the sword strap and pull the scabbard free from under him. Galator took the sword from Lask's pale hand, wiping it free of blood on the nearest soldier's uniform, the man recoiling from the griffin. Galator sheathed the sword and held it there in his talons. Looking down on it, he found himself torn between disdain and respect, not knowing which he felt, disgusted with his indecision. Part of him wanted to lay it back down upon the chest of its rightful owner, but it was that part that made him all the more furious. He curled claws around the scabbard and snarled to his men,

"Pick him up."

Several of the soldiers stepped forward, reaching down and hefting Lask up between them. As they did so, the griffin's hand went out to catch his head so that it did not fall back.

"Mind his head," snapped Galator.

The griffin clacked his beak and draped the sword strap around his neck to carry it, bending down for his soldiers to set the prisoner up on his back, laying him down flat along the griffin's spine.

"The rest of you disband. Scatter your tracks. Half will return to the caves, the others will join with the force in the south."

With that, Galator reached up to grab onto Lask's arm so he wouldn't slip, then opened his wings and leapt into the sky.

Chapter Forty-One

When Anarra returned with a band of soldiers to the battlefield, Galator's men had already gone, disappeared back into the forest as fast as they had come. Myranda walked among the Etherian soldiers as they began to gather the wounded, and spotted Forge, rushing over to him. He lay there gasping on the bloodstained dirt clutching at the spear embedded in his side. Myranda called a few of the soldiers over to carry him.

"Anarra," Forge whispered.

Myranda called for the Serin leader. The general reached into his shirt pulling out a crumpled paper and passing it over.

"Orders," he wheezed. "I'm in no shape to follow them."

Anarra nodded and instructed the soldiers to carry him back to the camp.

Myranda turned her eyes from their departure and looked to see Theramancer on the far side of the road. Several of the soldiers were trying to grab his reins and bring him in, but the horse was fretted, snapping and bucking, making it impossible for any of the men to hold him. He shrieked at them, kicking and cantering out of reach.

Myranda went toward them and told the soldiers,

"Go on. Help the wounded. I'll get him."

The men hesitated, exchanged glances, then trudged off back among the wounded. Myranda looked to Theramancer. The tall black horse watched her, nostrils flared, sides heaving. He was drenched in sweat and there were several bleeding wounds on his legs and flanks. He stamped an enormous hoof, the long hair around his ankles swishing.

"Easy," Myranda said, reaching out to him.

The stallion's ears swept back, wary. His head swung over, teeth snapping at her. Myranda pulled her hand back out of reach, then slowly reached out once more.

"Easy," she said again.

Theramancer held his head up, an almost arrogant and skeptical look, as if demanding what right she had to try to handle him. Myranda took a step forward and he snorted at her. The horse looked back toward the battlefield and Myranda got the feeling he was looking for Lask.

"He's not coming," Myranda whispered, and she could hardly keep her voice steady as she said it.

She offered a hand out to the stallion again. Theramancer didn't move, but he didn't snap at her. She went forward and reached out to touch his proud head and the stallion allowed her to take his reins. She led the horse back across the field and down the road to the camp. Once inside the perimeter, she tethered him so she could pull his tack off. Bringing some water, she rinsed the blood from his shining black coat and cleaned his wounds. The bleeding had already stopped, even in wounds that seemed deep.

"Are you immortal too?" she asked of the horse, giving a mirthless laugh. As she thought about it though, she said, "Why wouldn't you be? You are from the Immortals' land. You've probably been his horse for centuries."

Theramancer neighed deep in his throat, nudging his head against her. After she had finished cleaning him, she sat down and opened Lask's saddlebag. Inside, she saw the small leather box. The side had been crushed in the fighting and she had to give it a hard tug to force it open.

Inside was the Eurydicen seedling. The blow that had crushed the container had struck the sapling and the tiny tree lay broken amid the dirt. Its golden leaves were wilted and stained, the beginnings of its flawless grey bark scratched and scarred. The sight of it made the tears Myranda had held back well up and slide down her cheeks.

She reached in and carefully freed its tender branches from the dirt, pulling it back upright.

Knowing it was probably a lost cause, she nonetheless found a stick and some rope and staked the tiny tree back up, hoping that somehow its cracked trunk would grow back together.

Chapter Forty-Two

Myranda approached the long healer's tent and parted the flap. She saw the head surgeon, Salìt knelt there, hands stained in the blood of the woman he was tending, while the other healers bustled around him, handing him things and tending the others in the tent. One of them spotted her and said,

"You can't be in here. We need the space."

So, she withdrew. Not knowing what to do, she wandered the camp, seeing Anarra speaking to Astikin and Horace. She overheard the Serin leader say,

"Astikin, you know this country better than any of us. Ride as fast as you can, catch up with Ecthallia. Have her send someone to get Capperith. Give her this." Anarra passed Lask's letter into the mortal's hands. "Go, quickly!"

The mortal lieutenant took off at a run, heading for his horse.

Myranda watched him leave, and then returned to take a seat within sight of the healer's tent. She sat there as the sun sank low, until she saw Salit emerge to go over to the supply cart nearby. Myranda snuck past him and approached the tent. It was not as busy within, so she slipped inside, ignoring one of the healer's protests, and went over to see Forge lying sprawled on the floor, looking dead. His wounds had been tended, but she could see that the spear wound still bled a bit through the bandage. As she sat down next to him, he wheezed,

"Kill me."

At first Myranda thought he was still unconscious, talking in his sleep, but then his blue eyes opened.

"Kill me," he said again.

"I couldn't do that," she answered. "The pain will fade eventually—"

"I don't mean to put me out of my misery," Forge hissed. "I saw Galator fly off with Lask. He's probably already back at the caves. If I die, I will come back and my body will be healed. The sooner that happens, the sooner I'll be better, and the sooner I'm better, the sooner I can go after him."

Myranda hesitated.

"For heaven's sake, woman," Forge said, "You were out there killing the enemy like flies."

"That's different—"

"If you can take a life, why should another be any different?"

"You're his friend—"

"All the more reason to get on with it," Forge said with a grimace. "I'd die permanently if I thought it would save him. He would do the same for me and for you."

"Then you do it."

"If I do it, it's suicide. I don't think I would come back. I have to be killed by a mortal."

"How can I be sure you'll come back?"

"You saw Lask die here and he was fine. Don't see why it should be any different for me."

Myranda reached over and picked up the general's sword from nearby.

"For heaven's sake, girl, I don't mean butcher me!" Forge yelped. "Ask Salit for some poison or something."

"Right," she said, setting the sword down, "Sorry."

Despite his pain, Forge laughed.

"If you know about it," said Myranda, "Isn't that—?"

"I'm hungry," said Forge suddenly. "Do you suppose you could find me something to eat?"

For a moment, Myranda was about to demand how he could be hungry at a time like this, but then she caught on and went out of the tent. She approached Salit and the dark-haired surgeon glanced up at her.

"Did you need something, lady?" he inquired.

"Do you have any poison?"

Salit looked down his beak-like nose at her, skeptical and wary.

"Forge thinks that he would be able to rescue Lask sooner if I were to… well," she paused, not knowing how to explain that she intended to kill someone.

Salit reached into the cart and produced a bottle of dark green liquid.

"He's in quite a bit of pain," the healer remarked. "You could give him a bit of this in his drink to help. Only use three drops. Should you use any more, it could prove quite dangerous." He handed it to her with a pointed looked through his shrewd dark eyes.

"Thank you," Myranda said with a knowing nod.

She went to the nearest supply cart and picked out some bread and a bit of wine. She uncorked the phial and let a few drops fall in. To be certain it would work, she counted out six, then returned to the tent. Myranda was surprised that Forge could eat so ravenously, despite his grave wound.

"I miss normal food," he said as he picked the crumbs off his fingers, washing the bread down with the wine. "Regular rations are so dull. Our friend Capperith can make the most delicious turkey soup. And pastries— his cinnamon pastry is the best thing in the world. He's the captain,

The Immortal

you know. Strange really, that the army's captain is such a good cook, but—"

"What are you talking about?" Myranda asked. "You've been—"

"I'm carrying on a conversation with a very nice lady who came to visit a poor wounded soldier," Forge replied. "Very kind of you."

Myranda realized he was trying to trick himself into not knowing about the poison he'd just eaten. Though she knew nothing about Immortality, Myranda doubted that it worked that way. Nonetheless, she didn't say anything.

"I don't feel so good," Forge said. "Could be because I got *speared* today, but I think it might have been that God awful bread—" He broke off as a cough shook his body. He winced and was about to say something else when he coughed again.

"What did you do?" demanded one of the healers, rushing over.

Forge doubled over on his side, coughing and hacking and Myranda could only watch, horrified as he gasped for breath. Finally, he collapsed and she heard his wheezing breath finally stop.

"What did you do, woman?" snarled the healer.

Myranda sat still, at a loss, not daring to breathe. Salìt entered the tent behind her and stopped short. Myranda held up her hands, guilty. Forge lay still, pale and grey, thoroughly dead.

"Did I really kill him?" she whispered.

Salìt was kneeling at his side when a wind picked up outside and Myranda heard the soldiers on the perimeter shouting. The clamor was drowned out by the howling of the wind, and the tent door burst open with the sudden storm. Myranda looked out to see a shining silver mist swept along on the wind. It floated inside, writhing and coiling around Forge's still form. It seemed to flare brighter until it was suddenly drawn into his body and everything was still and dark.

Forge convulsed and coughed, sucking in a huge breath of air. For a moment he lay on his back gasping.

"Well that was not fun," he said, looking up into the concerned face of Salìt. He coughed again and then reached down to look under his bandages. "Yes," he exclaimed and smacked his belly where the wound had been.

"Are you alright?" Myranda whispered, stunned and awed.

"Considering I just died, I feel pretty damn good."

He went to get up, but Salìt held him there, inspecting the place where the wound had been for himself, not letting the general up until he was sure it was gone. Forge pushed himself up and groaned, stretching as if stiff. He reached down to get his sword, buckling it back on, and said,

"I'll leave as soon as I get a horse."

"I'm coming with you."

"I don't think so," Forge said, moving to go out the door, only to have her block his way.

"I just *killed* you so you could get better. Nobody else could or would have. You owe me for that."

Forge glared at her.

"So I *am* coming with you," she finished.

"Get your horse then."

Chapter Forty-Three

Galator entered the caverns, following the torch-lined passage back into the cliffs.

"You!" he squawked at a nearby soldier. "Come here."

The young man followed the griffin into a back chamber and Galator slid the unconscious Lask from his back.

"Strip his shirt and chain him up," said the griffin. He pulled the sword from around his neck and set it up on a rock ledge. "I will be back later."

The soldier nodded and saluted, not daring to protest as Galator padded away. Once the griffin had gone, he knelt down and undid the clasps of Lask's bloodstained shirt. He pulled it off, setting it up on the rock ledge by the sword, and then returned to pat down the prisoner's body, finding a small knife tucked into his boot. Satisfied he had been thoroughly disarmed, he dragged Lask over to fasten the manacles around his wrists.

As he was doing so, Lask shifted and the soldier leapt back with a yelp as he found those scarlet eyes upon him. The young man went over to get a hold on the end of the chain that looped up through a pulley in the ceiling, ready to pull it tight should Lask spring at him. Lask did not, but instead, brought a manacled hand to his head, the chain clinking, and winced as his fingers found the place the soldiers had struck him. His head throbbed with the drug they must have used to keep him unconscious.

"S-sorry," said Benac.

Lask looked over at him, both annoyed and curious as to why the enemy would bother apologizing.

"I'm supposed to chain you up," said the young man. "I could just yank you up there, but it would probably be easier if you'd stand."

"You're an awfully polite captor," Lask remarked. He looked the young man up and down, saying, "Hardly a soldier at all. A farmer, I would guess, by the state of your hands."

The young man just stood there, holding the chain, unsure of how to answer.

"I suppose the promise of Immortality would corrupt even the most honest of men," Lask mused. He got up and offered his hands to be hoisted up.

"It's not that," said the soldier, "I'm not a bad man—"

"Then why do you follow a murderer?"

"I was supposed to be married, see? In the spring," said Benac. "I was out with my girl one day and that beast found us, said he'd kill her if I didn't come with him. I went. I had to."

"And you think Galator would honestly remember your lady now, be able to find her, or even be bothered to go back for her if you should leave?"

The soldier hesitated.

"I'd set you free if I could," he said after a moment, "But there's no way I could get you out of here by myself. The best thing I can do right now is stay out of you Immortals' way and help whichever one is the biggest threat to me. And right now, friend, that's not you."

With that, he pulled on the chain and hoisted Lask's hands up about his head.

Chapter Forty-Four

Forge and Myranda rode to the northwest, following the information the search parties had given, hoping they were heading toward Galator's caverns. Clouds rolled in as night fell and the rain started, making the forest nigh impassable.

"Damn it all," Forge growled, knowing they'd never be able to see a thing.

He found a rock outcropping and slid from the back of his horse to shelter under the overhang. Myranda followed suit and sat down beside him out of the rain.

"Abysmal luck," muttered Forge. "We can't be far. Those soldiers were well rested; they hadn't been traveling that long." He ran hand through his wet hair. "Damn smart of him," he remarked.

"What do you mean?" Myranda inquired.

"Galator, up until today, was an incredibly predictable fighter. Every battle we fought, he'd have one charge, then another. Today, he had three, knowing that we would have thought it was over. Even more, the main attack came from the east. He knew we'd been concentrating our efforts searching the northwest; it was easier for him to assemble the largest of his forces in the opposite directions. The second charge came from the south. He'd been throwing us off all this time, sending his men to the south, making us think he was headed for the Gate, when really they were just circling back toward us." He shook his head. "I'm not sure he ever meant to attack the Gate. Spread our numbers out thin searching for him, lure us up here and make one swift attack to capture Lask." He gave an ironic smile. "That was his plan all along I'd wager."

"Why? To kill him?"

"I doubt it," Forge replied. "If he wanted Lask dead, he wouldn't have bothered flying off with him. He will be much more valuable to him alive." He paused, glancing over to her, then explained further, "There was about a hundred year gap between the time Lask's father was killed and the time Lask himself came to office. During that time, the kingdom was weak, far weaker than anyone would have thought. The Protector was always an important figure, but no one realized just how crucial it was to have someone carry that sword until there was no one who could. There was political turmoil, fighting, talk of war, no one to command the army, fear of Vortearigan's return.

There was such unrest then and it proved that to be without a Somadar could very well spell the death of the kingdom as we knew it. Thankfully, Lask came out of hiding and took up the job. Things have been much better since then, but that time proved just how fragile the kingdom would be should something happen to him. Galator knows this and knows that the king and the Senate would never want that to happen. Lask has no heir and his brother is certainly no candidate for the position. He is the last of the Somadars and the kingdom cannot lose him. If Galator plays his cards right, he can use Lask to twist the king and the Senate into doing whatever he wants them to." Forge looked over at her with a cheeky smile and said, "Which is why it is imperative we rescue his noble white arse."

Myranda gave a slight laugh, despite the situation.

"And we will," said Forge. "It's certainly not the first time I've had to, and knowing his luck, I doubt it will be the last."

The two sat in silence for a moment, listening to the pounding of the rain. After a time, Myranda said,

"May I ask you something?"

"Sure."

"Have there ever been mortals to enter Etheria?"

"A few," Forge replied. "Three, maybe. I don't remember, since it's such a rare occurrence. I'm not sure when the last one came through."

"What happens to them?" asked Myranda.

Forge glanced over at her from the corner of his eye.

"He invited you back with him, didn't he?" he said.

Myranda nodded and Forge smiled.

"Well," Forge said, "I imagine he plans to give you Immortality then."

Myranda's eyes widened.

"He didn't tell you about that," said Forge, realizing. "Right." He gave her a sheepish, guilty grin. "Don't tell him I told you."

"How does that work?" asked Myranda, fascinated.

"You don't say anything about it and I won't either, so I figure there's no way he'll ever— ow!"

Myranda had smacked him in the arm.

"You know what I mean," she said.

Forge glanced over at her, and then surrendered and said,

"The First were given a considerable amount of magic when they were Created, magic which was then passed down through their bloodlines. Anyone descended of them has a great deal of magic, though most never use much of it. Lask never has; doesn't have the patience for it and thinks it's a bit superfluous. I mean, why spend the time and energy to summon the magic to blast someone when you can just stab them?" Realizing he was losing the topic, Forge cleared his throat and continued, "That magic includes the ability to pass on Immortality. The noble will perform the Ritual with the mortal. Some people call it the Kiss of Life. They get themselves into this state where the magic can flow through them and then literally breathe the Long Life into the mortal. Apparently it's quite miraculous, though I've never seen it done, nor hardly anyone else for that matter."

Myranda took this in, both fascinated and nervous at the prospect.

"He loves you very much, you know," said Forge. "I can tell. He's only been around you a short time and it's been a hell of a circumstance, but he's always so happy around you. He's lived a lonely sort of life, only ever courted three women in all his years, and never once have I seen him look at somebody the way he looks at you. That, good lady, is a remarkable talent."

Myranda blushed.

"If I were you, I'd love him back with all the fervor he will love you with. Lask is a most loyal companion and I've no doubt he will make some lady a fine husband one day. Judging by the way he looks at you, I'd imagine you'd have an easy time catching him if you would have him." Forge smiled at her, then said, "But of course, as his best friend and brother by proximity, I must warn you: if you should do harm to his heart in any way, I will be obliged to hunt you down and make your life miserable for the rest of eternity." He flashed a broad grin.

Myranda had to laugh a bit at his ridiculous expression.

"I don't think you'll have to worry about that," she said. "I don't think I could stand to see him hurt."

"Good. Then I think you and I shall be excellent friends." Forge looked back out into the darkness, seeing that the rain had passed over them. He nodded. "I suppose we should press on then. We can't afford to waste any more time."

Chapter Forty-Five

Lask waited there with his hands chained above his head in the dank cavern, the air stale with moisture and smoke. Water dripped from somewhere behind him and the flickering torches only kept some of the shadows at bay. Lask had been somewhat surprised to see his sword resting on a rock ledge on the other side of the chamber. He couldn't decide if Galator had left it there to taunt him, or because the griffin still had a certain amount decency in him. After all, to handle the Somadar's sword against his will or without permission was perhaps one of the greatest insults a citizen could deal to that noble office.

He stood there in the chains for what felt like hours, until there was the soft padding of feet and he looked to see Galator enter the cavern chamber from the side.

The griffin walked around behind his prisoner, but Lask could not turn very far to watch him. He heard the shifting feathers of the griffin's wings and a rush of wind as Galator leapt past him with a bottle and chalice in his hands. The griffin sat back on his haunches and poured himself a bit of the wine, swirling it and taking a sip.

"The mortal's wine is really quite disgusting, but it will have to do," Galator remarked with a clack of his beak. "That is one thing your race has managed to do well."

"What do you want?" Lask growled, in no mood for games. "Why not just kill me on the battlefield? Why bring me here?"

"Kill you?" the griffin echoed. He took another sip, made a repulsed face, then set it aside. "Why Lask, you undervalue yourself. No, for some time now my primary objective has not been to return to Etheria and return to our war, but rather to capture *you*."

"Why?"

"It will take time for me to gather enough soldiers to challenge your army in Etheria, and in the meantime, I can't have you chasing after me at every turn. Besides, I hope to use you for more advantageous ends. While you are insufferably troublesome, I believe you will prove far more useful to me alive."

"Let me live and I shall be the death of you," Lask snarled.

The griffin's beak drew up in an amused smirk.

"We shall see, won't we?" he said. "Perhaps you also underestimate your king and the Senate. After all, you are the last of the Somadar line in Etheria. Without you, the kingdom shall have no Protector. I imagine they would value your life most highly, enough to perhaps grant me a few requests."

"They will not bargain with one who has terrorized their kingdom, no matter whose life you try to barter."

"I beg to differ," Galator hissed. "After all, you are among the strongest of the nobility. Without you, I imagine they will be much easier to persuade. Besides, it will prove even easier to achieve my plans should you beseech them on my behalf."

"I would *never*."

"Come now," said the griffin, "Depose my brother and make me the Rekan of my race and I will stop this war tonight."

"You have no place to ask me for anything," Lask replied, "Let alone demand I stage a coup on your behalf."

"Should you not think of your kingdom before your pride, Somadar?" Galator inquired. "You don't even have to slay my brother. Exile him if you like, just get rid of him. It could be done quietly. Why would you not take the chance to save your kingdom more bloodshed? I once told you that to ignore the voices of the ones beneath you would come at great cost. It has already had a price, let us not make it any higher."

"Perhaps there was a time I would have heard you," Lask growled back, "Had you come to me at the castle and spoken with me of your trouble. You lost any chance of that the moment you corrupted the first man against his kingdom. And now you have the audacity to insinuate that I am at fault for refusing you? You have rebelled, have slaughtered countless innocents, and have chained me, I who am your sovereign lord, in the dark like an animal. How dare you even *think* I would hear you here?"

"*That* is precisely what I hate," snarled Galator, pointing at him with a dangerous talon, "The way you and your fellows of power pretend to be so far above the rest. Look around you, Somadar. You stand a prisoner, far from your homeland. You are no lord here."

"Enough of your banter. Either take your chance to kill the one who vexes you or unchain me and I shall take mine!"

Galator let out a low, grating chuckle.

"You think you are so in control," scoffed the griffin. "If that were so, you would not have been taken by surprise. Your arrogance is what will undo you. So preoccupied with looking to the west, so sure that's where I was, you did not even bother to look behind you. And so trusting, so confident that no one would ever dare betray you.

How do you think I knew *exactly* where you'd be?" He turned his head back over his shoulder and squawked, "Trasiel!"

The soldier shuffled into the chamber, glancing up at Lask, but unable to keep his eyes there. He came to stand beside Galator, eyes on the floor.

"Have you any idea what you've done?" Lask asked of the man, voice quiet.

"Of course he hasn't," Galator answered, "That's the beauty of it. Now then, Trasiel, I believe I promised you something." He padded over the rock ledge behind Lask again and there was the clinking of something metallic. He reappeared with a small purse and handed it over to the solider saying, "Twenty gold pieces, as agreed."

Trasiel took it, holding it there in his hands as if it were a snake.

"Is that not all I promised you?" said the griffin. He paused, as if thinking. "Ah, no. I *did* promise you something else, didn't I?" He waited for the soldier to look up at him. "I promised to make you immortal like us."

Lask glanced to Trasiel, reading his face, the shame contorted around the hopefulness.

"Unfortunately," Galator said, "I lied. I have no way, whatsoever, to give you that." He gave a satisfied smirk. "But would you like to know the wonderful irony of it all?"

Trasiel studied him, confused, and Galator looked thoroughly satisfied with himself as he said,

"Lask here is perfectly capable of giving you Immortality with a single breath, and yet, he is the one you so willingly distrusted and betrayed."

Trasiel looked over to Lask then, horrified, at last starting to understand. Lask watched him, saddened that he had never earned the man's trust and that the griffin had taken such advantage of that.

"I'm sorry," Trasiel whispered.

"It's far too late for that, I'm afraid," said Galator. "Although had you paid a scrap of attention to me instead of watching Lask's every move, you might have realized before now that I can't be trusted."

Before Trasiel could even raise a hand to defend himself, Galator's hand whipped out, talons slicing over his throat. Trasiel fell back with a gurgle and died with an expression of shock and horror still on his face.

"You are despicable," Lask snarled at the griffin.

"But clever, you must admit," replied Galator, reaching down to retrieve the purse of gold. He gave it a shake, jingling the coins. "Now then," he said, sitting back on his haunches again, just out of reach of the growing pool of blood, "I believe I was discussing the terms of your surrender."

"Perhaps we ought to discuss the terms of yours," Lask growled. "Declare your surrender, submit to recapture, let me go and perhaps I can arrange a bit of mercy for you."

"Mercy," Galator spat, "A weakness and an embarrassment. You had your chance to slay me and look where your mercy has gotten you."

"Then I shall not make the same mistake twice."

Galator glared at him, emerald eyes level with scarlet; neither blinked nor looked away. Galator fluffed his feathers and broke gazes, turning his head back over his shoulder to squawk,

"Crowl! Bring in the other prisoner!"

A man stepped inside with heavy, stomping footfalls. He was a large man, sweaty and soot-streaked, carrying a long club by his side. He yanked on a chain, sending another man stumbling into the room.

Sifkin looked up at Galator and an expression of despair crossed his face when he saw Lask chained there.

"Now," said the griffin, striding over to him, "Perhaps you will not be so quick to dismiss my offer." He kept his eyes fixed on Lask, while raising a hand to brush his claws along Sifkin's face, trailing them down his exposed throat. "So young, aren't they?" remarked Galator. "Barely even older than infants of our kind. So weak, helpless, innocent. You wouldn't want to be responsible for his death, would you, Protector?"

Lask did not reply, keeping a steady, steely gaze on the griffin.

"I will give you til morning to think it over," said Galator. "In the meantime," he looked over to Crowl, "Why don't you see if you can persuade our prisoner? Do as you like, just don't beat him to death." He paused and gave a crooked smile, then amended, "On second thought, go ahead. It won't matter."

"What is this, Galator?" asked Lask. "Can't be bothered to raise a paw to torture your own prisoner or are you too much of a coward to strike the unarmed Somadar yourself?"

Galator's head whipped around, hissing at him, hackles bristling. He leapt back across the chamber. There was a hesitation in his movement, but still, his arm came swinging around to backhand his prisoner across the face. Lask spit at his feet and glared at him, both of them knowing the griffin had not been able to use his claws. Galator snarled and turned, stalking out of the room, taking up Sifkin's chain to drag him out in his wake.

Crowl swaggered across the chamber, hefting his club up over one shoulder. He paced around Lask, looking him up and down, but being sure not to come too close, for Lask wore a dangerous expression that dared him to come within kicking distance.

"I don't know precisely what the griffin wants you to do," said Crowl, "But whatever it is, you'd be a wise man to do it."

"And how could you, who have no knowledge of the situation, have any idea which of us is the wiser? As you continue to serve him despite the fact that a previous servant lies murdered on the floor, you are obviously not a very wise man yourself," Lask growled.

"Don't insult me," Crowl replied, and drew back his club to strike a heavy blow across the prisoner's back.

Lask glared over his shoulder at the man.

"You're one of them," said Crowl, "One of those undying monstrosities. It ought to be interesting to see just how long it takes you to die, how many blows it will take to beat the life out of you."

Another heavy thumping crack found its mark across his shoulders. Lask knew that Crowl stood directly behind him, making it impossible for Lask to strike out at him with his feet. The chains held his hands too tightly above his head, so he had no choice but to endure Crowl's punishment; every bludgeoning blow, every sickening thump, sending a slow burning ache up his spine. Perhaps it was the club falling on already bruised skin, or perhaps Crowl was swinging with greater vengeance as time passed, but it seemed the blows fell harder as they progressed.

Lask knew Crowl had managed to break the skin from the warm trickle of blood he felt traveling down the small of his back. From the pain that shot through him with each breath, he guessed the man had broken a rib or two as well. Lask just bowed his head, not giving his tormentor the pleasure of drawing a sound from him. It became a grim rhythm: the smacking strike, the aching pain in its wake, a momentary relief, then the pounding blow again elsewhere. His breath came shallow and ragged, unable to breathe from the tightness in his chest, the splitting agony that pierced him with each unwilling inhalation.

Sensing his prisoner's weakness, Crowl stepped to the side, nearer to Lask's bowed head.

"I could end it for you," he hissed, "One good crack in the head. Are you ready for death? Ask for it."

Lask just fixed him with an icy glower from the corner of his eye. Unsatisfied with that response, Crowl turned and dealt him a crack across the face.

"Ask for it," he growled.

Lask spat the blood from his mouth and held his silence. Crowl answered by taking a swing, catching his prisoner in the gut, knocking the wind out of him. Lask tilted his head back, wincing, trying to catch his breath, only to have the pain of his battered back and broken ribs deny him a deep breath.

Crowl stepped around in front of him, clapping the bloodied club with an appreciative hand. He inspected his work with a satisfied smile.

"Beg," he hissed.

Lask looked at him through the sweat-dampened strands of hair that hung in his face, baring his teeth both from rage and shortness of breath. He wrapped his hands in the chains above his head.

"Beg," Crowl said again.

"You will beg in the fires of Hell," Lask snarled.

He kicked off of the floor, hauling himself up on the chains, and lashed out at Crowl with an irate and agonized roar. He hooked one leg around his tormentor's neck, preventing his escape from the other foot that came driving into his face. Lask's boot heel shattered the man's nose, driving it into his brain. Crowl collapsed back over the fallen body of Trasiel, sputtering and gasping in his own blood as he died, the club clattering onto the rock floor.

Lask let himself go limp in the chains, entire body screaming with agony. A white-hot pain branded his back, his gasps sending a splitting fire across his sides. He could feel the dampness of blood on his back and tasted the salty sweetness of it in his mouth, feeling it trickling down his lip. In embittered hindsight, Lask found himself thinking perhaps he *should* have asked for death before killing Crowl.

The torches burned low, soon flickering out altogether, leaving him hanging there from his chains in the darkness. He could feel the manacles biting into his wrists, but didn't have the strength to hold his arms up straighter to relieve them. Every breath was a reminder of the pain, and each one carried the smell of blood, for much had been spilled in the room. He could no longer see the bodies on the floor, but he knew they were there, could feel their presence in the room, like a cold hole in the darkness, reaching out, but not pulling him into that sweet resting relief.

In the blackness, the snaking tendrils of despair wound around him, chilling his skin, tightening around his heart as if to strangle it. So much seemed lost in that cold, aching darkness. Stripped of everything familiar, so far from his home, Lask feared the darkness would never end, that the pain and *failure* would last forever.

And failure it was. Sworn to defend his kingdom, he had let live the greatest threat to it in centuries, and even now, having pursued him into another world, he had not been able to finish the task. If he had been stronger, if he had done things differently, none of it would have happened. His soldiers would not have been killed, Forge would not have been hurt, Myranda would not have suffered such torment.

The Immortal

The thought of Myranda brought an entirely new wave of regret. Though he had known her only a short time, Lask found himself thinking that he might have asked for her hand in marriage, might have given her Immortality so they could share eternity together. Much of his life had been spent alone; how different things would be with someone by his side, how much warmer the future would seem. There was so much that could have been.

And so much that had gone wrong. Fearing he would be crushed beneath the black silence, he drew an aching breath to whisper,

"Are you here? I cannot feel you as I once could, for things are so much darker in this world, so lacking in life, but you are the master of all things, all worlds and all that is between. You must see this place, and I pray you see me, alone and lost that I am. So much has gone wrong and so much do my mistakes cost.

"Perhaps it was my pride, or perhaps my fear, but whatever it was, I have been found sorely wanting. You charged me to do something that I have been unable to, and I can only ask that you do what I cannot. I have done what I thought to be right and it has only brought me here.

" The only strength I have is what you give me. Please, take this endless painful night and lead it to the morning. You have promised to undo the wicked, to give the powers of light the victory. I pray you will do so, for here I see only darkness. Let me feel your guiding hand, rescue me out of this night, and show me the path I must take to fulfill the vow I made to you and to my blessed kingdom. I live to serve you, but I cannot serve you without your aid."

Lask bowed his head in the stillness of the cavern and though his body ached from its wounds and his breath was stifled by the stagnant air, there was a peace that welled up in him, a patience that somehow found its way into the frenzied need for action, and he could now only wait for an answer.

Chapter Forty-Six

"There," hissed Forge, pointing through the trees to a light up ahead.

The trees thinned out into rocky crags and they could hear the distant crash of the sea. Myranda spied two guards pacing the perimeter. Forge had spotted them too.

"We need to get them," he said, "Their path should bring them this way. Snap their necks, that way no blood will get on their clothes."

Myranda looked over at him and Forge just growled, "This is no time to be squeamish!"

Sure enough, the two guards strode past their hiding place and Forge leapt out, grabbing one to haul him back into the brush. Myranda followed his example, latching onto the other, struggling back into the trees. She heard a sickening snap as Forge finished his work with the other, but was still grappling with her own. She hauled the man over, forcing him down into the dirt where she cracked his head on a rock sticking up out of the ground.

"Not quite what I had mind, but good enough," remarked Forge. "Strip him down and get into his clothes."

Myranda regarded him with a skeptical look.

"I won't watch," Forge replied, turning his back.

That had not been the reason Myranda was looking at him, but decided to just go along with whatever plan Forge had. She slipped out of her dress and pulled on the rough shirt and pants of the soldier, then stood up for Forge's inspection. He turned back around, having donned his own disguise, and didn't look satisfied. Bending down, he pulled the helmet off of the dead soldier's head and handed it to her, saying,

"Tuck your hair up in that."

Myranda did as he asked, seeing him reach down to pull the undershirt off the guard he had killed, balling it up and passing it over saying,

"Pad your shirt with that. Give yourself a belly."

Myranda gave him a strange look and Forge just patted his chest. Catching on, Myranda stuffed the fabric under her shirt to help conceal her bosom. Forge bent down and grabbed a handful of dirt, rubbing his fingers in it and reaching for her face. Myranda craned her head away.

"Hold still," the general grumbled.

Myranda obeyed, letting him rub a few streaks of dirt across her face before he rubbed the remaining grime between his palms and smeared it over his own.

"Right," he said, looking back out toward the entrance to the caves. "We'll saunter in and if anyone asks, we're bringing a report from one of the contingents in the south. They don't seem like a well-trained lot, I doubt they'll pay us much mind. Once we're in, we'll figure out where they're holding Lask."

"How do you expect to get him out of here?" asked Myranda. "He's kind of hard to miss."

"Forge isn't my real name, you know," he answered. "It's Josten. I earned the name Forge, from forgery. Maybe you'll get a chance to see why, though it will depend on the layout of the caverns and how much time we have. Speaking of time, we can't waste any more. Come on."

He stepped out of the brush and Myranda followed, walking along at his side, trying to seem inconspicuous. The two entered the caves and Forge flashed an amiable grin at the guards.

"What are you two doing here?" asked one.

"Bringing a report from the southern contingent," Forge replied and Myranda tried not to look surprised when a perfect Kwynnish accent came out of his mouth.

"You'll have to wait til morning to deliver it," answered the guard. "Galator's asleep."

"Just as well," Forge answered, continuing, "It's been an awful walk through this rain. Could use a good sleep before talking to him."

"Couldn't we all?" muttered the guard.

With that, they were inside. Forge followed the winding corridor, looking at ease and as if he knew exactly where he was going. Myranda noticed him glancing into the side caverns, but she didn't dare ask about it in case they should be overheard. Forge stopped short then and Myranda almost ran into the back of him.

"There's a guard up there," he whispered. "I'll wager he's guarding their prisoner." He glanced back at her. "There was a store room just back there. Go fetch a some wine from it."

Myranda wondered why, but decided not to waste the time to ask. She picked her way back up the slippery rock floor and entered one of the side rooms, selecting a chipped glass bottle and carrying it back to where Forge was waiting. He took it and sauntered forward.

"Evening, mate," he said to the guard. "Just bringing the griffin his wine."

"Galator hasn't been in this chamber for hours," Benac replied. "And I think he already had a bottle when he was speaking with the prisoner." He glanced back to Myranda. "I know you," he said.

"We've been here before," Myranda replied, lowering her voice into what she hoped sounded masculine.

"No," the soldier replied. "No, I saw you in Daeyi—"

Forge was on him in an instant, pinning him against the wall, dagger pricking his throat.

"Wait, wait!" Benac hissed before the general could slit his throat. "I can help you!"

Forge glanced to either side to make sure no one was around to see them.

"Talk fast," he growled.

"I never wanted to be here," the soldier said, "I know a way we can get out. The griffin has one of your soldiers prisoner as well. Sifkin, I think his name is. He's just in the next chamber. I can free him while you free your commander."

"What's this way out?" Forge asked, suspicious.

"There's a boat," said Benac. "Galator's been sending a few of us out for fish to help supply his soldiers. It's down below. It's small. We can sail it, just the few of us. Here." He reached into his pocket and Forge stiffened at the motion, but the soldier just produced a key. "You'll need that to unchain him."

"Give me your weapon," growled the general.

The soldier complied, unbuckling his sword and handing it over. Forge tossed it to Myranda.

"Go with him to get Sifkin," the general told her. "If he takes you anywhere other than where he says, kill him and get back here as fast as you can."

Chapter Forty-Seven

Lask awoke to a flickering light and a familiar voice saying,

"You look like hell, brother."

He opened his eyes to see Forge finagling the place where the chain was tied to the wall, working it loose to lower Lask's hands down.

"Forge," Lask hissed, "What are you doing here?"

"Saving your ass, of course," his friend replied releasing the chain.

Lask winced as he brought his hands down, muscles protesting at the motion. Forge came over to him, producing the key to unlock the manacles. Lask rubbed at his chaffed wrists, saying,

"You walked right into the middle of Galator's camp—"

"Should I have just left you here?" Forge inquired. "I know you said to just forget it if a rescue should prove too difficult, but you should know by now that I take that kind of talk as a challenge."

"Thank you," Lask said, with as fond a smile he could muster through the lingering pain.

"Looks like he got one of ours," said Forge, looking down to where Trasiel lay.

"No," Lask replied. "He was a spy."

"Sorry bastard," Forge growled. "That explains how Galator was able to pinpoint our location for that attack."

There was a motion at the cavern door, and Lask looked up to see Benac enter with Sifkin in his wake and yet another familiar figure.

"You brought her with you?" Lask growled to Forge.

"She insisted."

Myranda flung her arms around Lask, who yelped. Myranda released him as he muttered,

"Damn, woman."

"Sorry," she said, seeing the full extent of his injuries. She reached out to him, gentle this time, and Lask put his aching arms around her, the smell of her hair a most welcome reprive from the stale cavern air.

"As displeased as I am that you are in so dangerous a place," he murmured, "It is good to see you." He was reluctant to let go, but nonetheless relinquished her saying, "Come. We should not tarry." He limped over to the rock ledge to retrieve his shirt, pulling it on before bending down with a pained grunt to tuck his knife back into his boot. He took up his sword and looked to Galator's soldier.

"Changing sides are you?" inquired Lask.

"If it's not too late," Benac replied.

"Never."

"Come on," Forge said, sticking his head out into the corridor to make sure the way was clear.

"How do you plan to get us out of here?" Lask asked.

"This way," said Benac, leading them down the passage and around a bend.

The corridor was sloping down, the rock damp and slippery. Lask had to keep a hand on the wall to hold himself steady. All at once, there was a voice behind them.

"Hey!"

Forge looked back, speaking quickly,

"Just transporting the prisoners. Griffin's orders."

"You're the two that just arrived. I thought there was something funny about you!" The man called back over his shoulder, drawing in several other soldiers.

"Damn it," Forge growled. "Go!" He pushed them along down the passage, drawing his sword against the guards that came running after them.

Myranda took Lask's arm around her shoulders to steady him on the slick rock and she had to dig her heels in as he leaned on her. There was the sound of ringing sword blades and a scream that echoed off the stone as Forge dispatched one of their pursuers.

"Move faster!" the general grunted, kicking one of the enemy soldiers back.

"That might be a problem," Sifkin yelped.

They had rounded the bend in the corridor to find themselves face to face with three other men, drawn by the shouts. Benac raised his hands, having given his sword to Myranda. She promptly handed it back to him, too confined by Lask leaning on her to do much good with it. Benac drew his sword, lunging forward at the men who blocked the corridor. He felled one with a lucky swipe and Sifkin ducked down to grab the fallen man's sword, lashing out at the soldier who was charging him.

One of the enemy broke past and Myranda shifted free of Lask, grabbing the man's spear pole, giving it a yank to send him stumbling forward. Her elbow smashed into his face and she tore the spear from his hands, spinning it back to skewer him.

"Got more coming this way!" Forge called, seeing several more men appear further up the passage. "That boat better not be far, Benac!"

"Boat?" Lask repeated, looking stricken.

Benac broke past the last soldier in his way, slamming him into the rock wall and taking off down the passage, calling,

"Come on!"

He ran into one of the side caverns, Myranda leading Lask in after him. The stone floor gave way to lapping water and a small boat rocked there, tied off on a stalagmite. Benac leapt in and Sifkin followed suit as Forge came in, shoving back an enemy soldier.

Lask was standing there, eyeing the boat, glancing back to Forge and the soldiers that he was hacking at. The general stabbed one and smashed the other against the wall, then came running toward the water. Lask looked back toward the boat again.

"Do we really have to—?"

"Get in the damn boat!" Forge snapped, shoving him forward.

Lask stepped down into it, wincing and sank into an inelegant heap in the bottom while Myranda and Forge jumped in after him. Forge severed the rope with a swift swipe of his sword and Benac and Sifkin rowed them away from the ledge, as more soldiers came pouring into the chamber. They could hear them yell back out into the passage, calling for their fellows, shouting for Galator.

"Get down!" Forge shouted.

Everyone in the boat ducked just as two arrows came whizzing in at them. One splashed into the water beside them, another thunked into the mast. They started paddling again, passing out of the cavern and out onto the sea beyond.

"Get the sail up!" Forge exclaimed, stepping over Lask to reach for the ropes.

Myranda fumbled with the canvas, untangling it as the general yanked on the ropes, hoisting the sail to catch the brisk wind. He tied it off, then stepped back to the rudder.

They could still hear the shouts echoing out of the caverns behind them and Forge looked up to see a light on the cliffs high above.

"Get down!" he shouted again.

Several arrows whistled down from above, plunging into the water just behind them. The fierce, biting wind drove the small vessel quickly out of range, but looking behind them, Forge saw a dark form burst out of the caverns, wings splashing in the water as the griffin flew low over the waves.

"Get ready," the general called.

Galator caught up to their boat with a harsh caw and threw himself down at them, but Forge's quick sword kept those dangerous claws at bay. Myranda's spear pole caught the snapping beak as the griffin's flailing wings tangled in the ropes. Lask ducked a kicking paw.

Forge gave the griffin a kick, heaving him over the side. Galator floundered in the water, leaping back into the air after them. Before he could reach the boat again,

Myranda drew her arm back and flung her spear out over the waves.

It pieced straight through the griffin's left wing and Galator let out a screech, crashing into the waves with an enormous splash. The water frothed as he floundered, legs pumping to keep him afloat, wet feathers hanging limp around his face. Wounded, he had no choice but turn away from their boat and struggle towards shore.

"Excellent shot," Forge said with a grin, "Truly a wicked aim you have."

Myranda let out the breath she had been holding and allowed herself a satisfied smile. They settled back down into the boat, sailing off over the darkened water and leaving Galator's caverns far behind them.

Chapter Forty-Eight

Galator stormed back into the caves, dripping and shivering, wing dragging the ground alongside him.

"Incompetent fools!" he crowed at his men. "You let the enemy general just *walk into our camp*! My army cannot even stop five humans!" He swept back into his chamber, snapping at the nearest soldier, "You! Come here."

The man stepped up beside him, bracing himself for the worst.

"Pull it out," growled the griffin, offering his wing.

"Don't you think it would be better to—?"

"Pull it out!" Galator roared, snapping his beak just inches from the soldier's face.

The man complied, getting a hold on the spear pole and throwing his weight back on it to wrench it free. Galator shrieked, wings whipping, recoiling on instinct from the man. He snatched the spear from the soldier and snapped it in two, slinging the pieces back at the man.

"Send for the rest of our army," he snapped. "The enemy knows we are here and will surely march on us soon. We must be ready."

Chapter Forty-Nine

"What's wrong with *you*?" asked Myranda. Under the pale light of the coming dawn, they could see that Lask's snowy skin had taken on a miserable greenish hue. He hung over the side, clutching the rail in a death grip. Forge snickered from his place at the rudder.

"Oh shut up," Lask growled, casting an eye over at him.

"Lask has never been much of a seafarer," Forge explained.

"A greater understatement was never spoken," Lask muttered, looking over into the brownish water. If it were not for the fact he not eaten in over a day, he surely would have vomited into those waves.

Myranda ran a hand over his shoulders, feeling sorry for him. She reached up and coaxed his shirt off, Lask too preoccupied to wonder why she wanted it. She leaned over and dipped it into the water, wringing it out to start dabbing the dried blood off of his back. Her work stung, but Lask did not protest and stayed still, draped over the side.

"Does anyone know where we're going?" asked Forge.

"Head south," Lask answered, "We should be well away from Galator's caverns before making landfall. We'll put in further south and head toward the Gate. With any luck, one of our own patrols will find us."

Chapter Fifty

When they reached land, Lask was the first out of the boat. They hid the small vessel among the brush as best they could, then set off into the forest, heading east. Sifkin said he knew where they were, so the group let him lead. The soldier led them to the east then the south, heading for the heart of the forest where he said no one ever ventured, guessing that was where the Immortals would be hiding.

They walked on into the afternoon, having to stop and rest every now and then. While many of Lask's bruises had healed, it would take a bit longer to recover from broken ribs. They sat down under the spread of a hawthorn as the sun was beginning to sink low into the west. Sifkin wandered ahead a ways to try to get his bearings. He had not been gone long when the others heard him shriek.

They ran after him and burst into a clearing to see Sifkin pinned under the clawed foot of an enormous lizard-like creature. Twice as long as a man was tall, it stood over him with bumpy brown skin and a short silver mane growing from the top of its head and down its neck. An equally silver beard grew from its chin. It bared dangerous teeth down at the soldier.

"Kairn, no!" Lask called.

"You know zhiz man, Zomadar?" asked the lizard, looking surprised to see him.

Sifkin looked up, wide-eyed, shocked to hear it speak.

"Yes. He is with us."

Kairn flicked his forked tongue out toward Sifkin's face, then stepped back, releasing him from under his heavy foot.

"Fildahorr zaid you had been captured," he said. "Capperizh and ze rezt of your zoldierz came zhrough zhiz morning."

"Take us to the Gate," Lask asked of him. "I'll need to send someone to alert him and Ecthallia that we are here."

"Of courze. Come."

Lask and Forge followed the creature away into the woods, the three mortals trailing behind, more wary.

"What is that?" Myranda whispered to Lask.

"Kairn is a moranter," Lask explained. "They are one of the Immortal races that dwell here on Earth. They assist the Warauls with guarding the Gate." He paused and

Myranda got the feeling there was more say on the matter, yet Lask offered no further information.

Kairn lumbered through the woods ahead of them, leading them along no path that they could discern. As the woods were darkening into dusk, Myranda caught sight of what looked like a solid wall of brush and brambles. It was so thick, she could see nothing beyond it. Several soldiers appeared out of the surrounding woods saying,

"Commander!"

"General!"

They walked along the brush wall, Lask telling them,

"Send riders to Capperith, Ecthallia and Anarra. Tell them our whereabouts. Have Capperith send half a Serin to reinforce Anarra's numbers, then move east and subdue Galator's army there. Have Ecthallia move south and subdue his other soldiers. Tell Anarra to wait at her current location. Forge and I will return northward tomorrow to meet her, then move to attack Galator's location in the northwest."

The soldiers saluted then took off at a run to pass the orders along. Kairn led them to an opening in the brush wall where two warauls sat on guard. The pair nodded as they passed inside.

Myranda looked over the large clearing, seeing Etherian soldiers among warauls and moranters. Her eyes fell on the enormous arch at the other end. It was pale green stone, looking as if it had been hewn from a single giant piece. It had straight sides and a gently curving top, inscribed with strange symbols like she had never seen. Elegant vine knotwork was carved down each side, adorned in places with gold. It was an awe-inspiring thing, mysterious and inviting.

"The Gate," Lask told her.

Fildahorr came trotting over to greet them.

"It is good to see you, Somadar," said the waraul. "Word of your capture reached us last night. We were all most worried."

"Forge never ceases to look after me," Lask replied with an appreciative glance at his friend.

"Come," said Fildahorr, "I will show you to where you can rest for the night."

Lask and his companions followed the waraul across the clearing to an opening in the ground. It was crafted out of stone, like a well shaft, but instead of a straight drop, it opened down onto staircase. Myranda looked down it, seeing a soft golden light radiating up out of the hole. Lask followed the waraul in without a second thought, so she decided there was no reason to hesitate.

The stairs led them down into a stone corridor. It was supported by carved pillars and elegant arches in the ceiling, as if an entire castle had been buried under the ground. Fildahorr led them down the passageway, and Myranda could see several other corridors branching off on either side. The waraul led them down one nodding to three doors on the left.

"These rooms are free for your use, sir," he said. "I will send someone to bring you supplies."

"Thank you, Fildahorr."

The Guardian nodded and trotted back the way they had come, his nails clicking on the stone floor. Lask opened the first door and allowed Myranda to pass inside. Forge took the next one and Sifkin and Benac filed into the third.

"What is this place?" asked Myranda as she entered the room.

It was more spacious than she would have thought. Lush green fabric was hung in drapes along the walls, softening the hardness of the stone. There was a low table in one corner, and long pillows in the other, presumably to sit or sleep on.

"It is the Den of the Warauls," Lask replied. "It was built for them thousands of years ago when they were charged with guarding the Gate."

"It's magnificent," Myranda remarked. "Where is the light coming from?"

"Magic. A spell laid down by an Ancient."

There was a knock at the door before Myranda could inquire further. Lask answered it. A human soldier stood there bearing a tray of food and a waraul stood beside him, carrying a bucket in her mouth.

"Some supper for you, sir," said the soldier, passing him a tray.

"And some water to wash with," the waraul finished, setting down the bucket.

"Thank you," Lask said.

The soldier saluted and the two went back down the hall to fetch the same things for Forge and the others. Lask set the tray on the table then went over to the bucket. As he pulled off his shirt, Myranda was inspecting the food.

"What *is* this?" she asked, picking up a piece.

It was a stalk of something, with an orange stem and green leaves that were speckled with orange. Lask chuckled; whether at her ignorance or wary facial expression, Myranda did not know.

"It's keppàs," he answered, wringing out the washrag to wipe his face off. "Just eat the leaves. The stalks are brittle and have no flavor."

Myranda pulled off one of the leaves and slipped it into her mouth while he cleaned himself off. It was crisp and fresh, tasting a bit like a spicy carrot.

Lask finished rinsing and pulled his shirt back on, still a bit stiff from the beating he had taken the day before. He went and sat down beside the low table to help himself to some of the vegetables and meat there. Myranda saw a look of contentment, almost relief, cross his face at the familiar tastes.

"You must be terribly homesick," Myranda said, "Being in a world so different from your own."

"I am glad that it has not taken us longer to locate Galator," Lask admitted. He took a sip of the wine. "I miss my trees and the river. I miss the fresh air and the stars at night." He gave a sad sort of smile. "There is so much I'd like to show you. We are so close, but I cannot return yet."

"Soon," Myranda said, resting a hand on his arm.

"Let us hope."

Chapter Fifty-One

The next morning, Lask, Forge and the others set out back northward on a few horses Lask had borrowed from the soldiers stationed at the Gate. Being Etherian horses, they had excellent stamina, making the ride go swiftly. As they traveled, a group of six Etherian scouts caught up with them.

"News from Lieutenant Ecthallia, sir," said one of them, drawing his horse in alongside Lask's. "They have defeated Galator's soldiers in the southeast and remain there awaiting your orders."

"Have her hold her position there," Lask replied, "To ensure that what is left of the enemy force does not attempt to rejoin their fellows in the north. I plan to lead an attack on Galator's location tomorrow. I will have word sent to her of the outcome."

The scout saluted and he and his fellows turned away, riding off to deliver the message.

It was early evening when Lask and his companions arrived at Anarra's camp. She came out to meet them when they arrived.

"It is good to see you in one piece, sir," she said. "I have had our men keeping watch over Galator's location. As far as we know, he remains in the caverns. He sent riders out yesterday to the southeast, likely to call for reinforcements, but we apprehended them."

"Good," Lask replied, and told her his plan for the next day. "We will set out at dawn and hopefully be able to corner Galator at the cliffs. We should be able to make easy work of the few soldiers he has left at the caverns, and with any luck, he will not be able to flee this time."

Anarra nodded and set off into the camp to spread the word and begin preparations for the morning.

Chapter Fifty-Two

When Lask approached his tent that evening, he could see the lamp already lit inside and found Myranda waiting for him. He smiled to see her sitting there cross-legged, but noticed that she looked pensive. He unpinned his cloak and sank down to sit across from her asking,

"Are you alright?"

"I'm scared," she confessed, reaching out to take his hands. "It seems like a long time ago that Daeyi was burned, but it has been only a short while. I've seen so much since then, yet I could very well lose it all again."

Lask reached out and took her face in his hand.

"If you meet the griffin on the battlefield," Myranda was saying, "You could very well die. If—"

Lask leaned forward and silenced her with a kiss. When he drew back, he told her,

"I will not make promises to you I may not be able to keep, but you should know I have a very good reason to fight for my life. If I must die to save my kingdom, to keep you safe, then I will." He gave a slight smile and continued, "But I'd like to avoid that if I can."

"Do you have to go?" Myranda asked him, voice quiet. "You have such good soldiers, do you really need to—"

"I am bound by blood and honor to defend my kingdom," Lask replied. "It is not in me to stand at the back like a coward. Not even for you, my dear."

Myranda lowered her eyes to floor, having known full well that he would never agree to stay behind.

"I don't even want to think about tomorrow," she said, "What would happen if—"

"Then don't," Lask replied. "Let us not spend the night fearing for everything that might happen. No one can say what tomorrow will bring. Let's not waste our words on such dark thoughts." He slid in closer to wrap his arms around her, bowing his head to rest against hers. "For now, we have everything we need."

Chapter Fifty-Three

Lask was awake before first light. He roused Myranda, who went to dress and pull on the armor that had been arranged for her. While she was gone, Lask went out and fetched the large bag that carried his armor. He returned to his tent and set it out. He had pulled on the under pieces, the padded shirt and pants, with black chainmail along the arms and legs in the places that would not be covered by a plate. He slipped his feet into the plated boots, then buckled the greaves on over them before moving up to fasten on the cuisses over the top of each leg. They each contained three plates, attached underneath to allow them to shift over one another for better movement. He was just hefting the cuirass up and pulling it on when Myranda walked in.

"Would you like some help?" she asked.

"If you don't mind," Lask replied, turning to offer his back.

Myranda stepped up behind him. Like the armor at his legs, the cuirass was made of many small gold-toned plates, overlapping one another, capable of shifting, like long scales. The piece fastened at the back with a series of five large clasps, almost hinge-like in their design in the way they folded back on themselves, snapping into place and cinching the armor tight to his form.

"Thank you," said Lask. He fastened a belt around his waist, two sashes of deep red metal that supported a longer series of five plates, alternating red and gold, that hung down the front as a guard against gaps in the leg armor.

Myranda picked up one of the shoulder pauldrons to offer it to him. It, like the rest of his armor, was gold-toned, and consisted of three plates that could move over each other. Each was engraved around the outer edge with a swirling vine branching with leaves and blooms that resembled sunflowers. The upper one bore the seven-pointed sun of his family upon the curve of the shoulder. She held it out for him to slide onto his arm and fastened it beneath remarking,

"Surely this is not gold. It is far too light."

"It is a metal called ferratine," Lask replied as she offered the other pauldron to him. "It can be tinted to a variety of colors. It is very light, but also very hard. Very few things can pierce through it." He paused with a wry smile.

"Unfortunately, I would imagine that griffin claws are likely one of those few things."

"Splendid," Myranda muttered, picking up one of the vambraces.

Instead of taking it from her, Lask opted instead to pull on the black chainmail collar. It stretched diagonally across his chest and extended to either shoulder. His long fingers fastened the clasps so that the tall collar was closed to protect his neck. He then took each vambrace from Myranda and pulled them over his forearms.

"These are a little scary," she remarked, picking up his gloves.

They were black leather, but were sewn with movable plates along the fingers, each ending with a short claw-like tip. Lask chuckled and pulled them on replying,

"A hawk must have his talons."

Myranda picked up his sword, buckling the red leather strap across his chest, then wrapped his crimson cloak around him, pinning it there at his throat so that it draped behind him. She reached down and picked up his golden helm. It was cut back over each eye so not to limit his vision, while two wing-like shapes descended to protect either side of his face. Seven small rubies adorned the brow of it, while a simple hawk, wings flared, soared back along the crown of the head. A series of plates was attached to the back, defending the back of his neck, while still allowing him the free movement of his head. Seven sharp red feathers crested the top. Myranda lifted it up with a certain reverence and set it upon his head, almost as if it were a coronation and not the dawn of battle. She stepped back a bit after she had done so.

He was a fearsome, yet stately figure. There was an elegance to his armor, but a deadly precision, no part of him left undefended, designed to let him move with all the speed and grace of his normal motion. Myranda smiled a bit to herself and said,

"You look very nice, but I certainly wouldn't want to be in your way."

Lask smiled and stepped forward to her, reaching out to run a hand along her face. Myranda felt an odd mixture of fear and delight as those cold golden talons trailed down her cheek. Lask bowed his head and kissed her. When he pulled back, he murmured,

"If anything should happen to me—"

"Don't," Myranda said, laying a hand upon his armored chest.

"I have left orders for you to be taken into Etheria," Lask continued. "Please, go. You will be well cared for there. It is a land of great prospects and I have no doubt you would find a place in it."

"My place is beside you," she replied. She reached up to his face. "So don't go where I can't follow."

Lask bowed his head down to hers, whispering,

"Know that I love you and whatever may happen to this body, my heart will always remain with you."

He kissed her once more, then left the safety of her arms, turning to sweep out of his tent into the world of metal and blades beyond. He walked through the camp, the early light gleaming off armored bodies, the metallic sounds of footsteps and sword blades ringing through the cold air. He went to the edge of the camp where his horse waited.

Theramancer stood in full armor as well, in golden plates and black mail like his master. His breath fogged on the crisp air as he tossed his head, a single huge hoof stamping at the frosted grass. He stood like a thunderhead, black as a swift falling night, nickering and prancing, promising a swift vengeance to any foe that stepped in his path. It was all the groom could do to hold him still.

Lask took the reins and Theramancer planted his hooves, standing at attention for the commander to pull himself into the saddle. Once there, he turned his horse toward the field, trotting out to where the army was assembling.

They set out to the northwest, riding through the pale dawn. The force moved in uniform purpose, the metallic sound of their steps keeping time, like some foreboding clock counting down to the hour of battle.

Chapter Fifty-Four

It was still early in the morning when Galator was awoken by shouting ringing through the caverns. He was surprised he had slept at all, so nervous a rage he had been in the night before. He raised his head to see a soldier come tearing into the chamber.

"Lord Galator!" the man exclaimed, "The enemy! They have come!"

"Already?" the griffin screeched. He leapt from the rock ledge and bounded outside, opening his wings to flap up into a tall pine. In the distance, he could see the glint of the sun on armor and could hear the steady, deep, pounding of the drums. The stale wind carried the banners that spelled his doom.

Galator knew his reinforcements would not arrive in time. There was nowhere to go; his back was to the sea, to fly inland meant to soar over seasoned archers. He could

The Immortal

flee down the coast before they arrived, but he knew well that they would hunt him to the ends of the Earth.

"Sound the alarm!" he crowed back over his shoulder. "Make ready! All soldiers outside *now*!"

Chapter Fifty-Five

The Etherians came out of the trees to see their enemy scrambling out into the field before the cliffs. Not wasting a moment, Lask called,

"Archers!"

A volley of arrows arced up over the field, piercing into the enemy soldiers as they frantically tried to organize themselves. Lask's eyes found Galator perched up in the rocks out of the arrows' reach. Lask looked over to Myranda, who nodded, and then to Forge, who growled,

"Let's kill that bastard."

Lask unsheathed his sword and roared,

"Charge!"

The Etherians swept across the field like a gleaming wind, tearing into the enemy before they could form solid ranks. Metal rang against metal. Blood was sprayed like the sea foam far below. The mortal soldiers quailed and scattered before the fearsome vengeance of the Immortals who came down upon them like wolves upon sheep.

Lask hacked his way through the lines, blade striking down onto any enemy in his path. Forward, backward, his sword twirled, biting into flesh at every turn, carving his way across the field toward the crags. Most of the enemy soldiers tried to get out of his way, to leap out of the path of those dark, trampling hooves, to escape the judgment of that ancient blade, but few were quick enough. The sound of the screaming, the call of the horns, Lask hardly noticed as he burst through the ranks, pulling Theramancer to a rearing halt out on the cliff where Galator stood.

The griffin held his ground there on the edge, the cold wind stirring his feathers, carrying the scent of blood and metal. He saw Lask dismount, the steel of his boots clanging onto the stone. He stood there, the gold of his armor sprayed in red, the wind blowing his cloak out behind him, like flaring wings. His eyes blazed with the promise of vengeance, the fires of retribution, and for a moment, Galator thought of leaping from the cliff, of catching the wind to fly as far as it would carry him.

"Stand!" Lask roared, "And answer for yourself!"

"Now is the hour," snarled Galator, "When your kingdom shall mourn!"

Lask leapt forward and Galator lunged out to meet him. The two came together with a crash, the harsh grate of claws sparking off metal, the heavy thud of bodies plowing into one another. They collapsed out onto the stone, struggling in a tangle of kicking and clawing limbs, a slicing sword, a snapping beak. Lask rolled free, instantly on his feet, sword held up over his head at ready as Galator whirled.

The griffin's back legs threw him forward in a great leap, claws first. Lask darted to the side, sword sending the talons glancing away, and he had to duck low as the beak came tearing at his head. Lask spun his sword around, slicing it down the griffin's flank. Galator howled, flailing, and Lask was buffeted by his great wings. In the confusion, Galator flung himself over, pinning Lask down under two powerful forepaws.

Before he could swing his sword up, Galator threw his weight down on his paws, and the breath was driven from Lask's chest by the sheer force. He threw his foot up, kicking up into the griffin's gut and Galator staggered, but managed to pin down Lask's sword arm to keep him from scrambling free.

Lask pulled against him but to no avail. He kicked at the griffin again, this time reaching down with his other hand to draw the knife from his boot. He hacked at Galator's arm and the griffin squawked, drawing back on reflex. Sword arm free, Lask brought his blade up to keep the dagger-like beak at bay as he rolled back to his feet.

Lask stood ready, sword in one hand, knife in the other, waiting for the griffin's move. Galator leapt for him and Lask stepped to the side, but what he hadn't counted on was the griffin's tail thrashing back and yanking his feet out from under him. Lask crashed back onto the rock and just managed to get his sword up to stop the beak from snapping over his face.

Galator's hand came swinging down and Lask roared as the four talons pieced through armor and into his side. He brought his knife up, driving it into the griffin's shoulder and Galator gave a shriek of his own. The griffin wrenched his claws free with a loathsome twist and Lask gasped. Galator reared up, preparing to drop back onto him.

Lask took his sword in two hands, bracing it straight up. Galator saw his motion at the last instant and twisted aside, but still the blade pierced into his belly. The griffin collapsed out onto the cliff beside his adversary, wrenching the sword from Lask's hands and for a moment the two could only lay there, gasping.

Lask's mind screamed at him to move, but his body was slower to respond. He could feel the blood flowing from his side, running under the plates of his armor, onto the rock, following the cracks in the stone. It was difficult to breathe; he was sure the griffin had pierced his lung.

Gritting his teeth, he planted a hand to push himself up when Galator's arm came swinging over.

The diamond-hard talons pierced straight through the plates and into his chest, forcing him back down onto the stone. Lask let out a harsh cry, clutching at the talons embedded in his flesh. His hand closed around one of them in a vise-like grip, and when Galator wrenched his hand back, Lask clung on.

The talon was ripped clean out of the griffin's hand and Galator shrieked, curling his paw against him while blood gushed from the end of his finger. Lask gripped the talon in his hand, teeth bared in an almost inhuman snarl as he forced himself up to his feet.

Galator saw him rise and staggered up. Lask planted his feet, getting his balance. Galator hissed and lunged at him. Lask swung to the side, allowing the griffin to rush past him. In the instant Galator faced away, Lask flung himself onto the griffin's back, locking his legs in around the lithe body, and hooking an arm around his neck. Galator's wings flailed, beating at him, but Lask yanked his arm back, forcing the griffin's head up, then swung his other hand around to slice the talon across the griffin's throat.

Galator's body jerked and writhed, rearing back. His feet slipped as his life gushed away, sending him staggering with Lask still lodged on his back. Tawny wings fanned, holding them in balance for an agonized moment, until with a forlorn cry, both man and griffin toppled over the edge of the cliff.

Chapter Fifty-Six

Myranda's scream rang out over the battlefield, a horrified, piercing cry. She jerked her horse around, kicking her heels into its sides, galloping across the field and over the rocks. The mare stumbled, picking her way down the rocks as fast as the salt-slicked stone would allow. Reaching the bottom, Myranda leapt down into the sand, running along the shore, just out of reach of the water, past the tattered and blood-soaked form of what had once been Galator, until she stopped short.

A familiar figure lay in the sand, the waves lapping around him. Myranda stepped forward, as if in a daze, and sank down beside him. The sand around him was stained crimson, though the rhythmic waves pulled his blood back into their midst, in time making it disappear altogether. She extended a hand and brushed his dripping black hair out of his face, willing those now-familiar scarlet eyes to open.

He was peaceful in death, the vengeful mask of battle gone, looking as though he lay at last in content sleep. Myranda ran a hand down his face, shaking her head. Her breath trembled as she gathered him up to her, clutching him there, as an agonized cry escaped her. She bowed her head into his wet, salt-smelling hair, tears flowing freely down upon him, as she found herself plunged into that familiar, but terrible, darkness.

All the anguish of the past days, the utter loss of everything that mattered, came rushing back in like a black tide, the waves of that sorrow crashing over her heart, drowning the light that Lask had rekindled. There was no promise now, no prospect of tomorrow, for the only light that had remained in her world now lay in her arms, plunged into the darkness of death.

Through the clouded vision of tears, she caught sight of something lying in the sand beside him. Reaching over, her fingers closed around the long dark talon, hooked like the scythe of death. Its terrible point glinted in the light, promising the same fate if she had the courage to take it. Myranda knelt there, Lask cradled to her chest, the talon clutched in her hand. A shadow passed overhead, but she was too distraught to pay it any mind. Her eyes were drawn up though when a bright flurry of red and gold landed in the sand before her.

That scarlet bird, the one she had followed when all once seemed lost, stood there before her again, golden eyes glancing between her face and the talon as if demanding an explanation for the scene. His feathers flared around his head as he squawked, walking forward, elegant tail dragging in the sand. Myranda watched as the bird's long neck stretched out, laying his head down upon Lask's chest.

Pearly tears trickled from the phoenix's eyes, iridescent drops of grief that streamed down his face, rolling over battered armor and torn skin, faint golden sparks dancing in their damp trails. The phoenix wept, wings dragging in the sand, head bowed, and Myranda watched, both touched and intrigued by his grief.

Then all at once, Lask drew a great breath, gasping, scarlet eyes flicking open to find himself looking up into a red-feathered face.

"You're alive!" Myranda cried, crushing him to her. She heard Lask give a plaintive cry and released him, realizing he was still wounded.

He looked up at her, almost bewildered, raising a gloved hand to her face.

"Myranda," he whispered, "My love."

Tears still flowed down her face, though they shone with relief, the sorrow banished from her eyes by joy. She bent down and kissed him and Lask returned it, the passion rising out of the pain. Myranda pulled back and smiled down at him.

"You're alive," she said again, amazed.

"It is so good to be," he murmured, trailing his fingers down her face.

There was a squawk from beside them and Lask looked over to see Diem standing there, chest feathers puffed out with a satisfied gleam in his golden eyes.

"Help me up," Lask said and Myranda hauled him up to his feet. He bent down, still stiff and sore, and hefted the phoenix up on his arm. "Diem," he said, "I cannot thank you enough."

Diem let out a low coo, watching him with eyes that spoke of things to come. The phoenix bowed his crimson head, then opened his wings, rising to leave Lask and Myranda together there on the shore, and soared up until they lost him in the light of the sun.

Made in the USA
Charleston, SC
16 June 2012